LAST TALES

Copyright © 2001 by
Mildred P. Worrell

All Rights Reserved

Manufactured in the United States of America

ISBN 0-9713517-0-8

PRETTY CREEK PUBLISHING
P.O. Box 7933
Clinton, Louisiana 70722

LAST TALES

Passin' On in Southern Style

by
MILDRED P. WORRELL

Illustrations by Marsha Carmichael

PRETTY CREEK PUBLISHING
"ONCE YOU DRINK PRETTY CREEK WATER,
YOU WILL ALWAYS RETURN TO CLINTON."

DEDICATION

This book is lovingly dedicated to everyone who asked me to write it, helped me write it, dared me to write it. I hope it is only the first of many. I hope it makes you laugh and cry, in equal turns. I hope it reminds you of your own lives, the deaths and mourning occasions that are uniquely yours. I hope it reminds you of beloved figures from your childhood—and later— who have "Passed Over." Remember that the great William Faulkner said it best of the South's fascination—nay, obsession— with the past. Here, he said, "the past is not dead. It isn't even *past*." We live and have our being among that unseen—but not unfelt—band of angels, the beloved dead. Moreover, someday we'll join the band and exert ghostly influence over succeeding generations. We're all part of the tapestry. Some of our stories are more affecting than others', but it takes us all to make up the whole. I've been collecting stories all my life and don't expect to ever stop, so don't let the title fool you. There's no actual "Last" about these tales.

Heartfelt thanks to the legion of friends who urged me to "get on with it." You know who you are. More to the point, *I* know who you are, and I am so grateful.

Table of Contents

• • •

Preface 9

Last Tales 11
Sets the premise and tone of the book.

Grande Finale 15
Funeral music, good, bad, or absent. A grande dame's gospel send-off.

Burial Details 21
An Army officer is laid to rest with "full military honors," but somehow the Army wasn't organized to provide them without some "negative adjustments."

Don't She Look Natcherl? 29
Open vs. closed caskets, mistaken identity, "Baby-in-a-Box". The importance of a good final hair-do.

The Funeral Baked Meats 35
The fine art of "giving the funeral."

Making Arrangements 41
When it comes to funeral arrangements, sometimes you have to roll with the punches.

Uncle Ed Is Dead 47
Sudden (discovered) death in Texas.

The Most Fun You Can Have Standing Up In A Cemetery 53
Interpreting the history of our town through presentation of a cemetery tableau. Also: heat, wind, torrential rain, fire ants.

NIL NISI: THE ART OF THE EULOGY   67
What I have heard said, what I have said, what should never be said, what I couldn't believe I heard said.

DANCE ME DOWN EASY   73
Issy promised her sister she would die in her own room at home, surrounded by the things she loved, but then it happened another way . . .

FAMILY PLOT   83
East and West, New and Old South meet up in a family cemetery.

DEATH NOTICES   87
A tale of many funerals, social distinctions, and dark—and light—secrets.

PASCHAL FEAST   105
This one isn't even remotely funny.

AUNT LU, THE FUNERAL AUNT   111
Aunt Lu had buried most of her friends and kin, but she wasn't maudlin or gloomy. She understood death—and the proper way to say, "goodbye."

GRAVE HUMOR   123
An ongoing quest for the truly bizarre and/or tacky in last resting places.

COMPASS   133
A compass is something you use to find out where you are and where you are going.

Preface

Most of the stories I used for this collection are, if not totally and completely true, at least based on actual incidents or persons that come from real life. People tell me stuff, and I, having no shame, turn their confidences into stories. As my husband says, I "embellish" the stone, cold truth. I think it is safe, therefore, for readers to assume that no story can be taken at face value *except the following: Burial Details* (for which I thank the family who allowed me to tell this unbelievable tale), *Uncle Ed Is Dead,* and *Family Plot.* As bizarre as these three are, they are absolutely true. All the others have at least *some* elements of fiction—and fact—in them, so beware. There are stories that say plainly, "I am fiction," and essays that seem to be straightforwardly factual. It ain't necessarily so.

In addition, *Burial Details, Family Plot,* and the original version of *Last Tales* (then titled *Grave Humor*) have all appeared previously in *Country Roads,* the regional magazine (published in St. Francisville, Louisiana) that provides me with the opportunity to tell my stories every month God sends. My debt to the publisher, editors, and staff is immense. Many, many thanks to Jamie, Ashley, Ellie, and especially, Dorcas for faith and support. To make things slightly more complicated, I have used the title *Grave Humor* for a completely new story. I want to thank Father Graef of Holy Trinity Church in Shreveport, Mississippi, Ruth Quatelbaum, archivist of Phillips Academy, Andover,

Massachusetts, Jimmy Marston, Jo (Cataldo) Rousseau, and Julia Breitung for the factual parts of this tale.

For other stories grateful thanks go to the Charlets whose very excellent and professional establishment (Charlet Funeral Home) appears in various guises herein. Also to Darwin Hall for inspiring some of the anecdotes and to him and Sue Chaney for the little metal markers—and one cat. Also to Mark Kemp for the chicken and dumplings and for first alerting me to the military mess, Dewey DeLee for the camellia casket-piece, all "Shades of the Past" and support staff thereof, Lisa S. for the champagne, Rusty Bourgoyne for the phrase "white-knuckled recent post-seminarian," Paula, Gloria, Woody, Tip, and Ron for just about everything.

The design of this book owes much to Marsha P. Carmichael, most excellent friend and talented artist, and Cyndi Clark and Barney McKee of Quail Ridge Press. Good friends Edythe Lensing (who crossed state lines), John McConnell, and Kathy deGeneres read and proofed, rapidly and well. April Peterson kept me from going in the ditch coming home from Mississippi.

Thanks also to Marilyn Goff for invaluable help with publicity. Leo Honeycutt sat me down and told me how to promote this book, step by step. All authors should be so generous.

Posthumous thanks to Nootsie, Lytle, Ms. Clotiel, Uncle Ed, Maimé, Miss Lou Rist, Mr. T., Cousin Lois, assorted dead Lipscombs and Phillipses, and always and especially Mac, Nanny, and most of all, Mama.

My home country is the Felicianas of Louisiana, and denizens of that area are my people, but I think people everywhere—or at least everywhere in the South—are alike in the main, so even if you don't immediately know the "real" people who turn up dead in this collection, I'll bet you know someone very much like them, at least close enough to make a connection. So don't worry about who is—or is not—whom. As we say down here: "It duddn't matter."

Now Miss Bossy Britches will step out of the way and let you generous readers get on with the rat killin'. Here are *Last Tales*.

Last Tales

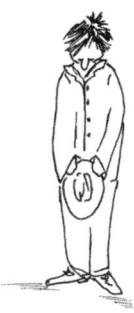

Mama always said, "There's never any event so sad that you can't find something funny in it." It was a philosophy of life in our family, actually, finding irony (if not always hilarity) in the tragic occasions as well as the pompous or the festive ones. It serves one well, especially in the navigation of the shoals and shallows of Southern small town social life—and death.

Now I am certainly not laughing at loss, not I, who grieve every day that my trinity of Mac, Mama and Nanny aren't here to fuss at and over me. I even mourn each of my dead cats, for Heaven's sake. Grief, however, should (and does, if you let it) temper with time. The knife becomes the needle that occasionally stabs your heart. I'm not talking about not grieving here. I'm saying looking at life from an ironic viewpoint pays off. You see a lot that's humorous, even more that's instructive. There is an attitude about death issues that treats the Grim Reaper and his attendant trappings, if not like a friend, at least like a well-tolerated acquaintance. I am a subscriber to this attitude.

The everyday coexistence, if you will, that my fellow citizens are able to share with Death was brought to my attention lately when, during a business call, a friend interrupted the business talk to ask that I check the Clinton grapevine to see if any member of a certain prominent family had recently died. It seems that she had called for a junior member of that family at her place of work and had been told the young woman was at a family funeral.

Naturally, she needed to know if she should send condolences.

I tackled the issue by going directly to the source of most information about death in East Feliciana (Caucasian sub-group), Charlet Funeral Home. My source there said, "Nope," there'd been no recent passing in the specified family. Thus, I was able to put a halt to that particular rumor.

My source also refused to accept my apologies for bothering her with such a silly request. "No problem," she said. "people call us all the time to ask, 'Is So-and-so dead?' and if they see our tent and an open grave in a cemetery, they call to ask who's dead and when is the funeral." Now think of that! Is that not full-service? That is full-service. How many times have I been about to attend a major social event and worried that if I encounter Mrs. So-and-so (which is highly probable at such an event) I won't know whether to ask after the health of Mr. So-and-so or not? It is a sure conversation killer to be told, frostily, that the person one has inquired after is, ahem, DEAD.

The cynicism and isolation of the late twentieth century have not made major inroads into the events of death in my little corner of the world. People honor the dead. You still see people pull off onto the side of the road or stand silently on sidewalks or in yards, men with hats in hand, when a funeral procession passes. People in the country know death is a part of life and understand John Donne's remark that "Every man's death diminishes me . . ." This doesn't stop us from observing the humor in such occasions.

I, like my father, am a connoisseur of funerals. He rarely missed one and took me with him from the time I was little. He was from a large family, and some relative or the other was always dying, so the occasions were many when I, dressed in my best, would be handed around to all the kin for general inspection. I didn't mind. The food at the wakes was always super, and my looks were much admired. Indeed, these were the only times I can remember when I, dead ringer for my Mama and all her family, was said to resemble Mac at all. He and I would laugh about this and tell Mama later to make her sniff at the improbability.

Last Tales

I grew up understanding the social and cultural necessity for funerals and all their attendant rituals. Consequently, I am always on the lookout for a good story when I attend. At one recently as I stood in a line to approach the widow seated under the "tent" (marquee), my paw was seized by one of the funeral directors who whispered to me to "Step up here onto 'X' and 'Y' (brother and sister-in-law, respectively, of the deceased, these already passed on, interred, and marked with stable, flat headstones) because I'd rather hold you up than pick you up." Of course, I was subduing chortles of laughter with extreme difficulty as I paid my—nonetheless sincere—respects. I have no shame. What can you expect from the child of a woman who herself fell asleep and snored (ever so gently) at the funeral of her husband of forty-four years? I looked over at Mama, and her dear little head was bowed in grief (I thought). Then, out came this snort. She had dozed off. (In her defense, I must say she had stayed at Mac's bedside pretty much day and night for thirty-one days. She was pooped.) The question then became how to wake her without provoking a startle response. Fortunately, I only had to touch her hand to get her attention. She looked at me a bit sheepishly and then brought her Kleenex up to her eyes to cover a giggle. I was forced to do likewise. No one else was even aware of the gaffe. I added this tale to my repertoire, which grows prodigiously. There are almost as many stories about deaths as there are deaths. I collect them. If necessary, I make them up. In this collection are some of each and all variants in between.

Due to familiarity in childhood, I've also never feared cemeteries. Taken with family to "visit" the graves and put flowers on them at intervals throughout the years, I developed a fascination with them that endures to this day. The creation of "Shades of the Past," which finds its way (highly fictionalized) into one of these stories, is a direct result of my childhood prowls through grave yards. Southern people have this "thing" about the "honored dead," even if we sometimes pay more lip service than elbow grease to maintaining their resting places, but there is a gentle movement in some places—like New Orleans—toward reclamation of the historic, crumbling burial grounds, and sometimes our honored dead are saved in spite of our neglect. There are stories about these occurrences, too.

It was impossible to keep from hearing Mama's admonitions on the day we laid her to rest up on Rose Hill. She had prepared me well for dealing with loss, grief, and mourning. Above all, there was the "nothing so sad that you can't find something funny" adage. There were numerous amusing anecdotes that came out of that occasion, too, for Ione was too colorful a character to have a dull funeral. I was surrounded by friends who each had their favorite memory of her, of her and Daddy, of other family gone before. It confirmed their philosophy about the end of life being one with life. The wonderful legacy that I've been given from my alert, storyteller parents is to be able to see life as a whole tapestry of all colors of thread, filled with details dark and light, and all very interesting.

I happen to believe that we will all be together by and by, and I guess that enables me to approach death with a certain irreverent reverence. Although all "death stories" are not funny, many are. Not all of the tales that follow are humorous, either, but they are deeply revealing of the way we Southerners encounter the various issues that surround our inevitable end. A very wise friend told me many years ago that people die as they have lived, and I have found it to be pretty nearly always so. Not in fear, not "whistling in the graveyard," but bringing flowers on Memorial Day, I offer these "Last Tales."

Grand Finale

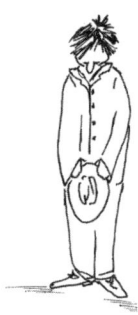

Music is terribly important at funerals. For one thing, it breaks the tedium of prose that often passes for tribute to the deceased—or the urging to amend one's life and follow (choose one:) God, Jesus, the Holy Saints, Allah, Jehovah, etc. (You get the idea.) For another, it gives everyone a chance to cry, and crying at funerals is a good thing, for the most part. I don't refer to loud, uncontrolled weeping, and I tend toward the Anglo-Saxon, Episcopalian style of discreet snuffling into a monogrammed white linen handkerchief myself, but crying is therapeutic, and a funeral is an excellent place to do it. One can cry about the loss of the one being honored, or the loss of another, or the loss of a job or a favorite piece of jewelry, if necessary, but it clears the soul to cry, so music is good, and the more evocative, the better. I find everybody says they hate music at funerals because it makes everyone cry, but we keep having it, don't we? Must be some comfort there.

In my mother's genteel, gentle Southern tribe of Methodists, "Abide With Me" is always sung or played, and I won't be the one to break the chain. At Mac's funeral, the talented church organist played the "Largo" from Dvorak's *Symphony to the New World,* which we recognize as "Goin' Home," a spiritual. It was so beautiful, and so beautifully played, that I have it on my list for my own obsequies. There are other Episcopal-type hymns I treasure, as well as old favorites from a more rural background. I think

Grand Finale

"Amazing Grace" amazing, and I loved it sung in the funeral scene in Alice's Restaurant, but it has been DONE, if you know what I mean. (The other funeral song from that film, "Songs to Aging Children," is on my list. It is practically unknown, sounds Judy Collins-ish, and is dear to me as a memory of the sixties and our goofy idealism.) My list does not include "Will the Circle Be Unbroken?" either, too repetitive, nor "How Great Thou Art" but I'm afraid there will have to be a sing-along wake for me just to accommodate all my other choices. I'd like a Black gospel choir to render "Precious Lord," and an Irish tenor to sing "Danny Boy," and Aaron Neville to do "Lay Down My Dear (Sister)Brother." I trust my survivors will be up to the challenge of all my musical requests! Never known for my singing skill, I do want to be sung out with lots of music.

The happiest and most serendipitous pairing of music and the deceased I can recall occurred at the death of one of my friends. Physically, she was unprepossessing, rather short, and, in her later life, rather stout. In every other way, however, she was formidable. Her attraction for me was simple. She reminded me of my own mother, whom I had recently lost. The two had, on the surface, few common traits beyond the fact that both were women of low stature but great personal charisma and with keen business sense. Nootsie was a wealthy, devoutly Roman Catholic mother of many children, from New Orleans (although with Feliciana roots, which she cherished), married to a successful businessman from the Nawth, a cradle Republican bleached blonde. Mama herself liked Nootsie's breezy spunk. Her favorite Nootsie story dealt with the image of the young matron, rather newly arrived on the local social scene, pouring coffee (or was it punch?) at a staid Garden Club tea, wearing a hat with a face veil and smoking a cigarette through the veil as she poured. It appealed to Mama's sense of the absurd, and, although the two did not share a friendship, they did each acknowledge the other as creatures of note.

By the time I swanned into her zone of influence, Nootsie was the established grande dame of the fledgling East Feliciana tourist

Grand Finale

industry. She and her family operated a successful inn on the outskirts of Jackson, the next town west of my hometown. I dived into tourism promotion on the rebound from quitting my day job, one of the ill-considered decisions I made in the days following my orphaning. Nootsie was my mentor. Her keen sagacity and excellent advice were poured out on me with generosity, as if I were one more of her zany, charming herd of children. I spent many happy hours soaking up her philosophy of the business. "What we are selling the visitors," she would intone to me as we each lolled in our seats in her elegant plantation home's parlor, "is not food or lodging or even sensation. What they are seeking from us is love!" She was a genius at providing the small touches that enveloped a visitor in the illusion of being part of the warm, charming Southern scene in a special, intimate way, not just as a tourist. We argued, mostly politics, often late into the evening. We had widely divergent views, and, during a particularly hotly-contested political race, supported different candidates and argued almost constantly. Her man was the choice of the moneyed, conservative "old" school. Mine was a recent immigrant, and I wanted change from the status quo. We didn't fall out, but it came close. This was the first time I recognized that I could develop a

Grand Finale

strong affection for, and loyalty to, someone with whom I strongly disagreed.

She had a massive stroke one autumn morning and was, for all practical purposes, dead when she hit the floor. I visited her stricken family in the hospital, having become pretty good friends with two of her children as we worked together on various projects. Naturally, they were shocked and devastated, but her strength was in them. After intoning the Lord's Prayer together at her bedside in the ICU, they said their goodbyes, and Nootsie was given back to God.

The planning of her funeral would have pleased Madame no end. It took place all over the house she had loved and lived in for nearly thirty years, was accompanied by lots of emotional outpourings, much good food and drink, and had all the hallmarks of a wonderful party, except that the great hostess was only there in aura. Some decisions were so easy. The funeral Mass would be held on the front porch of the plantation house, celebrated by a close family friend, and interment would be in the plantation cemetery nearby. Flowers were easily decided upon. Phone calls were made to friends and relatives across the nation. Even the weather was cooperative. It was cool and clear, one of those rare spells of true autumn weather we pray for here. At ten in the evening before the funeral it seemed as if every item on the list had been settled when the youngest two children realized that no one had obtained anyone to provide music. Did there have to be music? Of course! Who could be called at that hour? More to the point, who could commit at such short notice? I remember being present at the plantation for this crisis, but it is possible one of them called me, and we conferred by phone. (Memory can be unreliable.) At any rate, I offered suggestions, none of which were just right, for one reason or another. Then, remembering one of Nootsie's precepts (inclusion, never exclusion) I made a phone call, and the person on the other end of the line, doubtlessly slightly surprised to be asked, graciously accepted. The choice of song ("Just one," was the request) was left to him, since, as no

Grand Finale

accompanist was available, he would have to sing *a capella*. He said, "No problem."

And thus it developed that we gathered, a great heterogenous gang of us, in front of the beloved home of our beloved, departed friend in the crisp sunlight and participated in the celebration of her life, Catholics and non-Catholics alike joining in the parts of the Mass responses that were familiar. We were sad, but we were not bereft. Nootsie had given us so many memories, so much wisdom, so much fun! Her funeral was just like her, warm, unconventional, inclusive, and stylish. Tears flowed, but we smiled and felt satisfaction as the Catholics among us filed up for communion to the hauntingly beautiful strains of "Precious Memories," sung by a tall, handsome Southern Baptist ex-LSU football player who had been my man in the contested political race we had disagreed over so vehemently. The choice was eclectic, but all agreed it fit the occasion to perfection.

From the ideal to the ridiculous: Another colorful Louisiana character, struck down at the height of his political power, was also a devout Roman Catholic. The "anthem" sung as worshippers filed up for Holy Communion at his funeral was "My Way." Appropriate, perhaps, but tasteful? Hardly! Unforgettable? Certainly. An example to us all.

BURIAL DETAILS

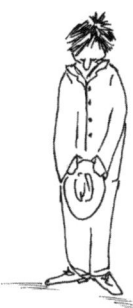

There were many men, and a few women, from our community who served with honor in various armed forces in "the Big One" (WW II), but none exceeded the rank and distinction of the deceased hero of this quirky tale. Mr. T, as he was fondly known, retired from the Army as a full "bird" colonel. He was a descendant of early settlers of the parish, had served many terms as an elected parish official, had myriad friends. It was to be expected that his funeral, coming as it did at the end of a long, full, and distinguished life, would be well attended. His devoted family, widow, two sons, two daughters-in-law, numerous grandchildren, and other relatives, certainly considered it only fittin' (as we say up here) that he be interred with full military honors. Among his family members are a Vietnam veteran, an Army nurse, and two currently serving officers in the Air Force. The request to the nearest Army facility in the western part of the state was made, as usual, by the funeral director, and all was in readiness. The church was full on a early winter morning. The family was gathering. The organ played. A cell phone, immured in the depths of a daughter-in- law's handbag rang. What?

All was, it ensued, not in readiness, and, as the congregation speculated on the absence of both of the colonel's two sons, the daughter-in-law retrieved the cell phone from her purse and obtained an update from her husband. Those nearby could hear his agitation, barely filtered by the phone. The service could—

Burial Details

indeed must—continue, he was heard to say, but the burial detail from Fort Polk would be delayed. With expostulations and not a few oaths, he explained the snafu to his wife who absorbed the data without comment. (The couple has been married a long time, and she knew the pugnacious nature of her man. It would not do to remonstrate over his language nor tone nor volume. This mess was a slight on the family honor. It was no time for moderation.)

Eventually, the pastor informed the congregation that, due to unforeseen circumstances, the interment of Mr. T would be delayed for an hour. All were to assemble at the Masonic Cemetery on the east side of town at that time. The widow and other family members thanked everyone for coming, assuring them that if the change of schedule was inconvenient, attendance at the grave side was not necessary, and that they would understand, etc., etc. After the sensation of the deceased's two sons, his only children, missing the funeral itself, few could stand to forego the burial. God only knew what would take place there! The attendees, paroled to go home and relax for about an hour, took the opportunity to telephone others who had not been at the church, and so the crowd actually increased for the cemetery event.

The burial, rescheduled for 13:00 hours, as we say in the military, was further delayed, but at least at the cemetery the two sons surfaced, and they passed among the others explaining what had occurred. There had been a, well, the kindest thing they could bring themselves to call it was a snafu, involving the burial detail. Seems there initially wasn't going to be any, as, at 09:00 hours that morning, only two hours before the funeral was scheduled to begin, the meticulous funeral director (a high school classmate and lifelong friend of the younger son) had called Fort Polk to confirm that the appropriate honor guard (composed of six officers to serve as military pallbearers, seven crack riflemen, and a major to present the flag to the widow) was on its way.

They weren't. The civilian clerk who had taken the request and promised the sending of the contingent only two days before said to the funeral director, "Oh (expletive deleted)."

Burial Details

"Lady," replied the funeral director, "you can call and tell those boys their daddy will not be having his military funeral, cause I'm sure not going to!"

Her call set in motion a frenzied scramble that began with the elder son (whom she called, fortunately, as he is the less volatile of the two) racing into the bedroom of his brother and sister-in- law, finding them partially clothed (getting ready for the funeral), not batting an eye, and saying to his brother, "Oh (same expletive deleted), they've screwed up Daddy's military funeral!" Consequently, the two brothers could not attend their own father's funeral because they both were pursuing the chain of command of the United States Army, up to and including the Secretary of Defense, to rectify the error.

The younger son, combat veteran of Vietnam, told me that he began by calling Fort Polk. He got a lieutenant who, wisely, decided the call was far above his rank and put a major on the line. The son told the major, "If you want to make colonel, I suggest you do just as the lieutenant did and pass the phone." He got a colonel on the line. The colonel said the commanding major-general was "in the field."

"Get him," was the son's response.

The brass at Polk professed themselves unable to rectify the problem, so the brothers got on the horn to then U.S. Senators John Breaux and J. Bennett Johnston and to Congressman Richard Baker. Through various phone calls all the way up to the offices of the Joint Chiefs, the Secretary of the Army, and the Secretary of Defense, they received assurances that an "appropriately constituted burial detail" would soon be on its way to Clinton, LA via UH1 (Huey) helicopters (3). An ETA of 13:00 hours was given.

The assembled mourners sympathized and applauded the sons' devotion to their father. Tho' the hour advanced, and no Hueys were seen or heard, no one left the graveyard. A news crew from a Baton Rouge television station that specialized in exposing scandal (and had had a fruitful crop to expose in our

Burial Details

area) was on hand to film whatever occurred. They hoped for outbursts of fury and a confrontation to liven up the 5 o'clock news. Finally, at 13:30 hours the "whup-whup-whup" familiar to viewers of M.A.S.H. and the evening news as the sound of big helicopters was heard. Folks strained to see, shielding their eyes to better pick out shapes in the pale winter sky.

Then the choppers (three, as promised) were overhead, hovering, seeking to land. The ever-prepared funeral director, never himself having been in the military, but having seen plenty of TV helicopter landings, raced to a cleared place on the east side of the cemetery and began signaling them down. Unfortunately, the pilots chose to set down on the far side of the cemetery in the Haynes pasture, a Clinton landmark more associated with parking for the pursuit of privacy while courting than for military exercises. Also, a stout fence separated the pasture from the cemetery proper. The muddled soldiers disembarked, and someone went to locate a ladder. Amazingly, one was quickly found, causing the younger son to remark, "That's the first damn good luck we've had today." The burial detail scaled the barbed-wire fence,

Burial Details

and led by their commanding E6 (a sergeant, far cry from the person of the rank of major that the Army promised to send), proceeded to the shade of an oak tree to assemble and confer. It soon became obvious to those who pressed closer that the dozen or so young people lacked experience in serving as a burial detail. There was no bugler among them. They had brought a "boombox" to supply "Taps." When the tape deck was turned on, however, rap music, chiefly remarkable for a pounding bass rhythm line, boomed forth. The tape was quickly changed.

The brothers noted that not one of the young people held a rank above corporal and that all looked bewildered, but grateful for the appearance of any military contingent whatsoever, and not wanting to offend the soldiers who were straining to perform at their best, they kept silent as the session of practice stretched into many minutes. Finally, salvation came in the guise of the retired major who served as the R.O.T.C. instructor at the local high school. (He'd been invited by the funeral director to bring some of his cadets to observe a crack military burial service.) This officer took command, and, in a short while, the service began.

Mostly, my informant says, it went fairly well, although the sergeant was forced to employ hand signals to cue the playing of "Taps," and during the firing of the twenty-one gun salute the volleys were so randomly fired that his daddy may have gotten a thirty-one gun salute, or a ten gun salute, who knew? Finally, the interminable process of folding the flag that had covered the coffin was completed, and the R.O.T.C. retired major, as the ranking officer present, presented it to the shell-shocked 83 year old widow, for whom it had been an even longer and more stressful day than she could possibly have anticipated.

As is our local custom, all the mourners were invited back to the house for food and drink, and there, able to relax at last, the soldiers of the burial detail began to tell their stories. The group met the "new" Army's standards for diversity. There were male and female, African-American, Hispanic, and plain old white soldiers, but all of them were young, and of their number, only two

Burial Details

had ever participated in a military funeral before. Moreover, they had been practically kidnaped, seized from performing their usual weekday jobs and ordered to grab a clean green uniform (not their dress blues) and climb aboard. One of the young women was terrified the whole trip. She had never even been in an airplane before. She was a clerk in the commandant's office, and the MP's came and seized her. There were mechanics from the motor pool, nurse's aides from the base infirmary. The only criterion for inclusion beyond random selection was whether the potential individual approached had a clean uniform ready to wear. There was protracted confusion about whether to wear or bring the uniform. Wear it. No, the uniform would be wrinkled after the long helicopter ride. No, wear it because there would be no place to change clothes at the cemetery. The debate raged around the bewildered young people. Finally, they were herded aboard the Hueys and transported to Clinton, where they were landed in a cow pasture and had to climb a fence to get into the graveyard. Their heads had not yet stopped spinning, but they did appreciate the food and kind remarks of the family, especially the widow, who kept saying, "The poor little things!" Everyone was very kind to them, and all relished the stories. The bemused E6 was heard to say, "I'll bet my wife thinks I've been kidnaped. She and I watch the soap operas together every noon, and I didn't even have time to call her." (He was handed a cell phone.) The young soldiers asked innocently, "Who was that man we just buried?" They figured he must have been somebody very powerful to have occasioned the wild recruitment and helicopter deployment.

On the return trip, one of the helicopters, having stopped in Baton Rouge to refuel, broke down, and the entire crew had to be loaded into the remaining two helicopters. When this information was relayed to Clinton, Mr. T's widow went into a serious praying mode, afraid the two remaining Hueys would be overloaded and crash, but, thankfully, neither that nor any further mishap took place. The brothers had contained their (locally famous) tempers. Mr. T had received a military funeral, by God, one

Burial Details

which no one who had been there (or who was told about it) would ever forget.

"It took our army months to send twenty-three choppers to that mess in Bosnia," my informant tells me. " I got three of the (expletive deleted)s to Clinton in under three hours." No brag. Just fact.

There would be many letters exchanged over the shocking lack of concern exhibited by the Fort Polk commandant when faced with the snafu his civilian clerk had effected, but those of us who knew Mr. T know he thoroughly relished all the fuss and feathers his receiving "full military honors" entailed. His son said he could just see him up in Heaven, telling my Daddy and Mr. Joe Felps (old vets like himself), "Now, boys, that's what I call a grand funeral!"

Don't She Look Natcherl?

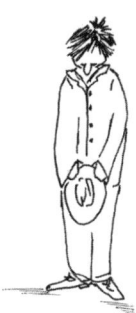

It was drummed into me from the time I even knew what a funeral was: No open coffins.

No gazing at the dearly beloved recently departed. Mama was adamant. "They always say," she'd quote, derisively, 'Don't she look "natcherl"?' Hell, no, she doesn't look 'natcherl;' she looks dead because she is dead!"

And that was, for many years, that. I accompanied Mama to any number of wakes and funerals. She had this tactic that she used to avoid an open coffin, if the family'd been so ignorant as to have one. She'd go right up the aisle at Charlet's or Rabenhorst's (the only two funeral homes we ever attended in those early days) and then, as she got close enough to the bier to see whether the lid were closed or not, if it were open, she'd veer off at an angle and approach whichever member of the bereaved family was farthest away from the offense. Then she'd hold ground there, in the midst of the family, until all members were forced to approach her position. She'd extend sympathy to all in earshot. Then she'd leave. If one of the family tried to draw her up to the coffin for one last look at the dear one, she'd gently demur with a murmured, "I'd rather remember (him/her) as I saw (him/her) last." This was usually sufficient. When the family member insisted ("You never met my new husband, Ione," was one cousin's plea

Don't She Look Natcherl?

that went outside usual practices) she remained in control. ("And now is not a good time," she cooly replied, extricating her arm from the grip of her kinswoman. "Oh, look. There's Mrs. Blah-blah-blah . . ." and we were off in a cloud of Kleenex.)

"Ma," I'd remonstrate, "you hurt their feelings."

"Baloney," she'd reply. "They'll forget it if I did." This was another of her closely cherished—and frequently passed on—dicta, that the shock of a loved one's death put the ones left behind into a sort of null state that would be only vaguely remembered in the months and years to come. "You feel dull, Baby," she'd insist, "just dull, and the grief comes in waves." She deemed it her duty to prepare me for the rituals and ordeals of losing loved ones because I was born when she was approaching middle age, and in the natural order of things, she might not even survive until I was grown. Just as I had to be trained in good taste in clothes and encouraged to get a good education so that whether or not I married, I would be able to support myself, so must I be schooled in the proper way to manage deaths.

"Don't you even think about letting people look at me dead!" she told me too many times to count. She was vain, and she really did want people to remember her—as she truly wanted to remember them—as they appeared in the vibrancy of life.

Then Nanny died. Nanny was our housekeeper, and she was also one leg of the triangle of adults who raised me. There were only Mama and Daddy and Nanny and me. Of course, there were dear friends (whom I thought of as "aunts" or "uncles") as well as actual relatives, but our tight circle was those three adults surrounding the Baby, me. Nanny was the first of my "parents" to go, and, actually, she was a good one to go first because she was devout and never feared death—greatly different from both Mama and Daddy, who were total chickens in the face of their own illnesses. Anyway, when I was a young adult, recently married, Nanny died after a relatively short illness. We knew she was dying, and we were as "prepared" as you can get, but we were all still devastated. My husband was somewhat less upset than Mama

Don't She Look Natcherl?

and Daddy and me, but it was a big blow to him, too. He, however, had the excuse of having to work on the night of Nanny's wake, so it was just the three of us going into the funeral home. This was in the late sixties. It was not at all the usual thing for white people to go to a Black-owned and operated funeral home then, but we loved Nanny, and we had plenty of Black friends, so there was no question. Daddy got hung up in the lobby, meeting and greeting. He was the most gregarious man I ever knew, never met a stranger, and he always shook hands and slapped backs as if he were running for something. Funerals and wakes were his favorite social events besides dances, and he was in his element. Just Mama and I made our way up to the front of the room where the body was.

The coffin was open. I heard Mama utter her favorite expletive under her breath. There was no escaping it this time. Nanny's family and close friends surrounded us, and we were escorted up to the casket. There was this woman in there. She was in a pinkish lilac crépe something with a high neck. Her bosom was formidable, and her hair was piled forward on the top of her head. I lost use of myself for a moment and thought, "This isn't Nanny. We're at the wrong wake." I even turned to Mama and said, "Ma, this isn't Nanny." The attending crowd began to murmur, "Poor Baby. She doesn't even know her own Nanny," and one woman began to fan me. It was bad.

After Mama extricated us from the ensuing debacle and we were safely home, she dithered, "It's my fault. I should have prepared you." Then she proceeded to tell me how morticians in general, and those of the Black subset in particular, liked to fix up the corpse. Not content to have the body appear as in everyday life, undertakers liked to gild the lily. Nanny, in life, wore her hair pulled off her face in a bun to one side at the top of her head. In life, she wore comfortable clothes with reasonable necklines and went "loosely corseted." In her coffin, she had a wholly different look. The embalmed and embellished Nanny wasn't herself. Not recognizing her wasn't my fault. "I do hate open cas-

Don't She Look Natcherl?

kets!" Mama expostulated, yet again. I saw what she meant.

"But what," I demanded, "was she wearing? I never saw Nanny wear anything like that, not to church nor to my recitals . . ."

"A shroud, Baby. That was a shroud." Then she went on to explain shrouds, twentieth century variety, that they are pastel colored nightgowns with a sheer bottom. Then I had to swear—all over again—that not only would I never let anybody see her dead, I also would never put her in such a garment.

When Daddy died, I didn't let anybody—not even Mama—look at him. We just trusted Charlet and buried him.

Then there was the time when one of my husband's relatives died, and my best friend, Paula, went with us to Texas for the funeral. I'd tried to explain the layout to Paula, who was relatively a funeral virgin, not experienced as I was. The funeral home Ron's family used was a fine, big one in the small town nearest his home, and it was housed in a grand new building. Unlike the funeral homes I was used to, there was no private area for the family in the "viewing rooms." The term "viewing room" meant just that, because caskets there were invariably open. It was foreign territory to me. The funeral director, named (I am not making this up) "Billy Ray," was flamboyant. On a previous occasion, he'd met us at the cemetery to mark Ron's father's prospective grave site attired in a red sport coat, blue pants, white shirt, and a stars & stripes tie, and it wasn't the Fourth of July or anything. He also sported possibly the worst toupé in the western hemisphere. I was used to the extreme dignity and conservative attire of the Charlet , Rabenhorst, and Richardson crews, and I was much taken aback by Billy. I warned Paula that he was a bit exuberant for his profession, but, as she and I sat in the central lobby (where you could, in those more corrupt days of the 1970's, still smoke) he came bouncing in, clad all in shades of gray, introduced himself all over again (Billy never seemed to recognize me) and blurted, "You ladies gotta come see this. Babyinnabox. Purtiest li'l thang you ever did see."

Don't She Look Natcherl?

He really meant it. Stupidly, like cattle, we put out our cigarettes and followed Billy into one of the other "viewing rooms." This one was dark, not yet set up. On a table was a tiny white satin box, maybe 18 inches long. Before we could collect our wits, Billy flipped on the lights and whipped the top off to display—just what he'd said: a baby in a box. Dead. Very.

"Ain't she just the purtiest li'l thang? Stillborn. Mama was all doped up. Never saw her. I fixed her up. Gonna show her to the Mama. Ain't she purty?"

I—to this day—don't remember how Paula and I got away. The next thing I remember is being outside in the car demanding that Ron take us into the next county (wet) to a liquor store. We allude to "The Baby in a Box" whenever we want to denote some particularly egregious lapse.

So Mama died, and I did let just a few, very close friends see her in her coffin, after we'd gotten George Charlet to put red lipstick on her to replace the modest pink they'd initially used. ("That was it," George said. "I knew she didn't look just right . . .") She was dressed, for her ultimate social occasion, in the very becoming lavender dress she'd worn to her last birthday party. It happened to be crêpe, but it was a dress, not a shroud. Her friend and hairdresser for thirty years had given her, just a few days

Don't She Look Natcherl?

before she died, a fresh permanent wave. "That was a good wave," she told me after fixing Mama's hair for the coffin. "Ione's hair never looked so good." This decided me. A good hair day when meeting your Maker is not to be wasted, so that cinched my decision to risk her eternal wrath. We all looked. We all agreed. She looked just like herself. Really. Dead, of course, but pretty damn natcherl.

FUNERAL BAKED MEATS

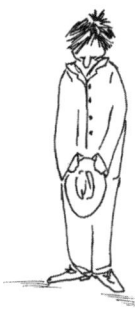

"In 1949 I gave four family funerals. One of them was my own mother's. In 1961 and 1962 I gave three more. In between, I gave God knows how many and how many later, one or two a year." This was my own Mama talking. I heard the refrain often, usually when some other woman of her generation professed herself completely at sea at the challenge of hosting hoards after the last rites for some relative. Hosting friends and family fresh from the grave side was just one of those duties that went with being female and Southern in Mama's opinion. You just did it.

It devolved on us to be in the host role (by us I mean not only Mama, but Daddy, me, and, most importantly, Nanny) because Mama was the last of her mother's large family to remain in the place of origin. All the aunts and uncles and cousins had migrated to other seaports, mostly New Orleans and the Gulf Coast, near enough to still feel an attachment to the ancestral home and want to be buried there, but not resident. Moreover, we had a big, old house, suitable for entertaining, and we had Nanny. Nanny was our cook-housekeeper, and her cooking was legendary. Her pies, cakes, fried chicken, ham, potato salad, rice and gravy, sweet potato casserole, and biscuits were outstanding, and what are all of those but classic Southern funeral food? She could cook for a crowd of thirty without any effort; indeed, she really preferred to cook for a crowd. Not, you understand, that she would ever have to supply all the food all by herself. Not in our

Funeral Baked Meats

community. Even though Aunt Leila and Aunt Em and all the other dearly departed might not have lived around here for many years, they were remembered, and friends and distant relatives would feel honor bound to contribute food offerings.

I grew up taking the art of funeral giving pretty much as a regular event, certainly not strange or threatening. My memories of the activities surrounding funerals are calm and positive, not unlike other parties and dinners we were used to hosting. It could be said I learned the "how to" of this aspect of Southern female code in the same way I learned how to do all the other sundry tasks expected. My tutors began with something I could do pretty easily and expanded from there. My earliest job was to log in the food as it was delivered to the kitchen from various sources. Of course, this was well after the big funeral year of 1949 when I was just two-going-on three. That one, I barely remember, but by the next halcyon year I was fully employed. The science of tagging the various baking or refrigerator dishes with coded stick on tags had not been developed. We used freezer tape and written descriptions. I got quite good at descriptions out of self defense because when all the hoo-raw of the dining and departing was over, Mama and Nanny would sit me down and force me to decipher whose bowl was which. There are only so many ways to distinguish baking dishes, unless you've been very observant in the beginning. Any tell-tale crack or chip would aid me. If we couldn't be sure, Mama would always let me off the hook by saying, "Well, if we can't tell, probably she won't be able to, either." We never got in trouble, so I can conclude that it worked. From that point, I developed phone skills, substituting for Mama with the ladies who'd call offering to send something. This require keeping track of what had already been received, as well as what was in the promised pipeline. By age eighteen, I could handle this with aplomb. Nothing to it.

Of course, there were some offerings we liked better than others. There would always be at least three bowls of potato salad besides Nanny's, which I liked best in all the world. Jo Hobgood

Funeral Baked Meats

made hers with olives, and Mama adored it, but I was picky. Somehow, Mama always saved Jo's contribution for last. There is an art to saving stuff after one of these soirées, never doubt it, and Mama was the past master of it. Usually, however, there was precious little left over. Our family were prodigious eaters. At one of the later family funerals, one of Mama's first cousins sat at a little low table for two hours while his wife steadily brought him food. This was extreme enough for us to remark upon it, but not all that out of line. Rarely did any substantial portion of food survive what my Daddy called "the attack of the starving Lipscombs." This was all to the good. Leftovers were a problem in our household. We had but the one freezer, and it was full of stuff we'd put in there and forgotten until it was unidentifiable and inedible. Better we should eat it all up and start over. After all, we had Nanny. What need had we of leftovers?

The world changed radically after Nanny died, the first of my trinity of beloveds to go. Once her fine hand was lost, we had to rely on the kindness of others—and the Chicken Shack. Mama learned to stir pots enough to survive, but she'd never make a chef, not even a cook. We never stopped hosting the after-funeral receptions, though. They were our obligation. As the family wanting to be planted in the ancestral soil thinned out, we expanded to host the last dinners for friends' dear ones. Daddy's own funeral was monumentally well provided for, but oddly, I don't remember a whole lot about it except that it was in June and hot. When Mama died, ten years later, we gave the whole funeral at the house, and it is indelibly etched in my brain.

Friends—she had so many—came from all over the area. We laid her out in the parlor like it used to be done before funeral homes arrived here in the late 1940's. Her own father and brother had been waked at home, and she'd said she felt comfortable with the custom, so we resurrected it for her. She'd loved her house beyond all reason, every creaking floor board and unevenly hanging door, and it just seemed right to have all her last rites in that setting. It was comfortable for us, too. We had access to

Funeral Baked Meats

beds and restroom as needed, and we were at home. The kitchen filled up with friends, most bringing food, and everybody stayed to exchange stories. It is the custom here for various people to contribute not only prepared foods but paper plates, Cokes, etc. It is not the custom for anybody to send beer, wine or other alcoholic beverages, but often, if they are available, such are happily consumed. This was the case at Mama's wake. We would send to the store for beer, and it would be drunk. In the meantime, the food, Cokes, and paper items rolled in freely. My husband, not raised as I was in the rigid etiquette of the Southern funeral, was manning the phones. People would call, express condolences, blah, blah, blah—all extremely kind—and then they would ask what we needed. He told them.

It was not long before one of my closest friends took me aside. "You need to know this," she whispered. "There's kind of a problem." My husband's requests for beer were causing scandal in some quarters. He, being forthright and practical, had expressed our most pressing requirement. (I could hear what his justification would be: "Bunny, they asked what we needed!") Unfortunately, such candor went against the code. Alcohol could be consumed but never mentioned. I had a tiny word with him. That was all that was necessary. Meanwhile, the food stacked up. There were ten bowls of potato salad, six casseroles, three huge aluminum roasters of baked beans, and eight whole, baked hams.

I passed by the chair where my husband was on the phone and heard him say, "O.K., if you don't feel comfortable about bringing beer, just don't bring ham!"

When we moved into The Big House after extensive renovations eighteen months later, we thawed out the last of the baked hams and served it at the party. My husband understands freezers.

No account of giving the funeral would be complete without citing the all-time favorite food we enjoyed. A pot of chicken and dumplings prepared by a friend of Mama's barely made it into the house on the day of the wake before being attacked by all and

Funeral Baked Meats

sundry. My very dignified (usually) and proper friend from New Orleans did everything but mow down rivals for the delicious concoction. It made such an impression that, only having tasted it once almost twenty years ago, it still is the hands-down winner she and I discuss whenever we talk food. The lady who made it passed on shortly after Mama, so we've had a real problem getting any more. Now word comes that the lady's daughter has perfected the art of preparing this near-Heavenly dish. We are laying plans. We hope to be able to get ahold of some without resorting to actually giving a funeral, but whatever it takes, we will do.

I have been to probably two hundred funerals and to "back to the house afterwards"-es almost as many. I have personally hosted at least ten. They are very much alike, no matter the circumstances or the parties involved. Some are, of course, more solemn than others, but invariably, the food is good, the reminiscences are mellow, and the fellowship is uplifting. Rarely are there conflicts or bad behavior. I am reminded of Auntie Mame's oft quoted declaration that, "Life is a banquet, and half the poor suckers are starving to death." These unfortunates should come by the next time one of us gives a funeral. We know how to do the job right.

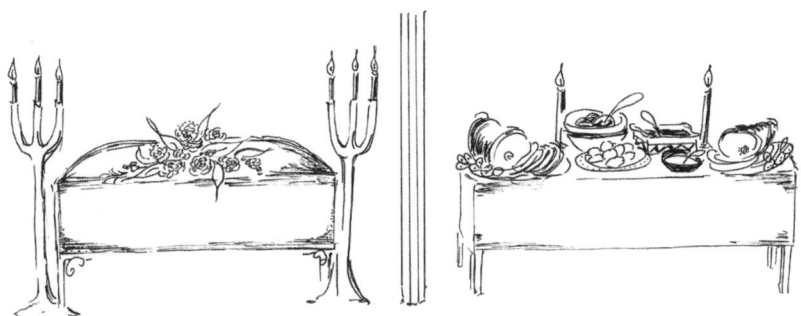

Making Arrangements

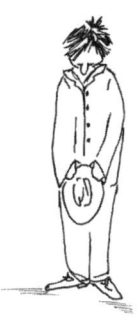

The phone was ringing as I opened the front door. I threw my purse on the table and dived for it. It was Vera, and before she ever got the words out I knew. Miss Mathilde was gone.

"Mama's dead," she said and then she sobbed. We were expecting it at any time. Her mama had been in a decline for several months, and just before Christmas she'd gotten so bad, she'd had to go into the nursing home up in Flora, Mississippi where she lived. Vera'd made the three hour trip up to see her almost every week, and, just two days before we'd met for lunch, and Vera told me then it would not be long. "She knew me when I got there, but, when I went to leave, she'd turned her face to the wall." As an orphan myself, I felt the awful weight of pending loss. Now it pent no more.

The first thought I had was that I couldn't drop everything and go north with my dear friend. A very important business meeting was on my agenda for the next morning. I was deep into working up to my apology when Vera cut me off. "I know you can't get loose until tomorrow evening," she said. "It's all right. Clark is on his way down to pick me up. We'll go back up there tonight."

"Are you sure you'll be O.K. with Clark?"

"Molly, I love Clark. I've never stopped loving Clark, and

Making Arrangements

Clark loves me. If only . . ."

"If only he hadn't fallen in love with the florist . . ."

"Grover prefers 'floral designer,'" she began.

"And I'd prefer that my old college bud Clark hadn't fallen in love with a man and left my old sorority sister for him."

"Please Mol, that's all water under the bridge." I was instantly ashamed. Vera's mama wasn't cold yet, and I wasn't helping my friend at all. I apologized. Then I had to apologize again because my own husband, Ray, was in Montana hunting.

"But I'll call him. He'll get a plane out. He can fly into Jackson." The rest of the conversation went a little better, at least I behaved better.

"Oh, Molly," Vera said just as we were hanging up. "The funeral won't be until Saturday, and it's supposed to snow up in North Mississippi tomorrow." Swell.

• • •

I called Vera as soon as I got under way driving up I-55 from Hammond. My meeting had gone long, and the clients insisted on taking us out to a late lunch at Trey Yen, so it was late afternoon by then. The skies were gray and the clouds looked like snow clouds, but down here it was still not cold enough to snow. I devoutly hoped I'd make it to Flora without incident.

"How are you?" I asked.

"I'm alive," my friend replied. "Don't ask for more. We went to the funeral home and made the arrangements."

"You sound awful. Was it awful?"

"Awful enough. I'll tell you all about it when you get here."

"Is the house full of people?" I enquired. Vera hadn't gotten around to doing anything about renting or selling her mama's home yet. She paid Miss Mathilde's maid to go in once a week and keep it clean, and she'd stayed there when she went to visit. I expected half of Flora to be camped out in the big old living room.

"No, I sent everybody home. I needed to be by myself. You

just get on up here. You're the pal I need right now."

"I'm coming, honey."

"And Molly, stop in Jackson and get some gin. There's not a thing to drink up here but Bourbon."

"Already tended to. I packed carefully."

"I hope you brought Mr. Mink. It's fiercely cold up here and getting ready to snow, I swear it is."

"Is the fire going?" Vera's house has a huge fireplace. It was her daddy's pride and joy.

"Fire going, plenty of wood in, and I lit all the space heaters in the bedrooms. Just come on."

• • •

We sat up pretty late, didn't, after all, drink much. Ray always says, "Grief and the grape don't mix," and that goes for the grain and the juniper berry, too. Vera kept making drinks and not drinking them, letting the ice melt until the thing was undrinkable. Then she'd get up and make another. I started to fuss at her for wasting good gin, but caught myself. She did recount the whole funeral home episode, and it was true black humor.

Vera said, "I'd already called Jack Morris and set up the appointment before I left home. He was terribly sweet and apologized over and over that he was going out of town today and couldn't meet with us himself, but I was really glad. Mama never did like him, ever since he jilted me my senior year. I would have been really uncomfortable around him. He said his assistant funeral director, Marvin Peters, would meet with us, and I said, 'Fine, but I want you to tell him I don't want to go in that room with the caskets.' I had to do that when Daddy died, and I have a horror of it. So he said that would be fine. Marvin would show me some books so I could pick out the coffin from the books. At first I thought I'd handle that O.K., but I lay awake all night last night thinking about it, and by ten this morning I was a wreck.

Making Arrangements

Clark and my cousin, Billy (He's the one who's a banker.) went with me, and, in the car, I kind of had a fit, and I made them promise they'd go in the room and pick out Mama's casket. I should have known that would be more than they could manage.

"Well, when we got to the funeral home, Marvin met us and took us into an office. He is a really big man, played defensive end for Ole Miss, took up preaching, now he's a funeral director. He's very professional, kind and very soft spoken. He tried to show me that damned book first thing, but I had a little reprise of my hysteria, so he and Billy and Clark went off into the casket room, and I was left to wait it out.

"I know a half hour went by, and I was so bored I was almost reduced to looking at the casket book. I'd already read all the 'Pre-need Planning' brochures. Then Marvin came back. You could tell he was a little afraid to come close to me. I had acted pretty crazy, I guess. He just sort of hovered, and he was holding his hands folded in front of him like preachers do, you know?"

I nodded. I was spellbound.

"'I'm afraid,' he said, 'the gentlemen have come to an impasse.'

"I'm afraid I said a bad word. That shook Marvin. He twitched, but he kept composure.

"'Now don't get upset,' he cajoled. 'If you will just come and stand in the door of the casket room . . .' (Gesture of sweeping me out the door.) In my head I was cussin', but I was good.

"Well, of course, I wound up having to go in there and pick out the damn thing. Then he asked me if I had brought Mama's clothes, and, of course, she hasn't worn anything but cotton nightgowns for over a year now, and just last month I gave all her clothes to Goodwill, so I broke down again.

"Billy had to debate every price of every item of the bill, and Clark was so nervous, I thought he was going to chew the rug. We finally got out of there. I signed my life away, and I still don't have a shroud for Mama."

"Not to worry. We'll think of something. You did very

Making Arrangements

well." This lone survivor stuff is hell. I know. Still, it beats having to contend with critical siblings when the hard decisions have to be made. Give me control any day. Your friends can provide the closeness and support. That's why I was here for Vera. She'd been with me every step when my parents died.

There were other glitches in the funeral planning. There always are. It snowed. Boy, did it snow. It snowed that night (Thursday) and the next night, and I was scared Ray was going to miss the funeral, but he made it. Vera had wanted her mama's casket flowers to be camellias from the yard. Miss Mathilde had a green thumb and a yard full of bushes, and, indeed, the bushes were covered with blooms, but it snowed and froze, so the blossoms were all ruined. For once I was glad of Grover who said he would take care of the flowers and for us not to even worry. He really is very nice. It is small of me to resent him and Clark, but my memory is too long. I remember like it was yesterday the night Vera called me to tell me her marriage was over. It was the very worst, 'way worse than a timely death. Oddly, Miss Mathilde handled the divorce and scandal so much better than Vera or any of Vera's friends. Clark was wonderful to her in these last years, and Grover, too. Of course, Miss Mathilde had lived a long time, and she could roll with the punches.

Besides all this, the Methodist minister was brand new, and, because Miss Mathilde hadn't been able to get to church for over a year, he didn't know her. When we talked to him about her, what a fine lady and talented gardener and devoted churchwoman she'd been when she was able, he wasn't hearing us. Since he didn't give off the right warm vibes, Vera fired him. "I won't have him getting up there and saying he didn't know my mother," she said as we left his office. "I hate that worse than anything at a funeral, everything but the music."

The Saturday was very cold, low twenties with a wind that cut like a knife. The service was all at graveside. Miss Mathilde hated funeral homes, and we surely weren't going to the Methodist Church. The husband of another friend of Vera's was

Making Arrangements

an ex-Roman Catholic priest, and he conducted the service out of the back of the Methodist hymnal. We all said the Twenty-third Psalm and the Lord's Prayer together, and Marvin (who has a fabulous baritone voice) led us in singing "In the Sweet By and By," Miss Mathilde's favorite hymn.

The sun came out as we were standing there, huddled in our warmest coats, and it shone very briefly on the simple wreath of mixed camellias that lay on Miss Mathilde's coffin. Grover had driven down to his sister's home in Hattiesburg and cut over two hundred blooms from her bushes, which, because it hadn't gotten below freezing down there, were perfect. He explained that you have to have triple the number of camellias to start with because they are so fragile and apt to shatter when you wire them. He'd done a masterpiece. The wreath was breathtakingly beautiful, all pinks and roses, Mrs. D. W. Davis cereal-bowl sized blooms mixed with tiny, pink Debutantes and big Purple Dawns. Such a tribute.

"I think it was a nice funeral," Vera said shyly as we drove home. "The flowers were beyond lovely, and the casket was fine, and even if I didn't think I could bear music, I'm glad Marvin sang."

"And we didn't need that snotty old preacher at all," I added, "and we didn't freeze."

"And we buried Mama in your beautiful Dior silk kimono. That was so sweet of you, Molly."

"It was the least I could do," I demurred. "Truly, Vera, Miss Mathilde got put away in great style."

"Mama'd like that," she replied softly, looking out the car window. The snow began to fall again.

Uncle Ed is Dead

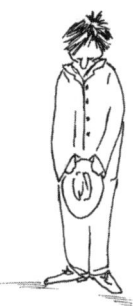

I'll say right off for the record that I don't like Texas. The best thing that ever happened to me—a really wonderful husband—came from there, and for that, and for his character, I'm grateful, but I never got along with his parents, and I hated just about every minute I spent there, and I go back only when it is absolutely necessary, and I count the moments until I can come home again. At the time of this event I am about to describe, we were on our way outta there. We had one more stop to make, a visit to Ron's last living uncle, Uncle Ed. A widower and a more recent grass widower, Ed lived alone in the same village he'd always done. He had some heart trouble, but he was an active man, a worker, by God. He'd tell you quick: he loved to work.

"Do I have to go in?" I begged Ron as we pulled up to the house. Both of Ed's cars and his truck were there. No chance I could see that he wasn't at home. It was just past one in the afternoon on a warm Sunday in March.

"Now that'd be real tacky, your sitting in the car."

"He never talks to me anyway," I continued to protest, weakly, but I knew R. was right. It would be pretty low to snub the old man like that. I sighed and dismounted from our van. I was thinking that if I had to hear banal conversation about hunting and "Do you have your garden in yet?" I'd gag.

Ron hopped up on the concrete stoop and rang the door bell. Still reluctant, I hung back. I remarked to myself in my head that

Uncle Ed is Dead

you can always tell the sound of a truly empty house. This house was still the way no house with living things in it ever is. Inside, a phone rang. Ronny said, "That'll be Aunt Bernice calling to warn him we're coming."

"She could save her nickel," I groused. "He's obviously not here."

There followed one of those marital discussions when each party has a vested interest in being right. I declared he might have been picked up by his latest lady friend. R. declared that it just didn't add up. I drifted around the side of the house and looked under the carport. The glass doors into Ed's den were closed, but the drapes were open. I went up and peered in. The reflection of the truck behind me distorted the impression, but it looked like Ed was lying on the floor. It passed quickly through my mind that he was lying under the chassis of a truck. Crazy how your mind works when the raw reality of something won't be accepted, and you make up a story that won't be as shocking. Ed was dead, of course, not lying under a truck but just on the floor of the den.

Well, this took the rag off the bush, as Mama used to say. I wandered back to the front stoop and told Ron he could stop ringing the door bell, and then, of course, he had to go see. He went in and, as they say in the police procedurals, determined that life was extinct. I got on our car phone and called 911.

It was at this point that the situation went from tragedy to black comedy, for it is true that if you are sufficiently cold-blooded to see it—and I usually am—people throw over social restraint at the event of death and some act plumb funny. I began the farce. I could not describe to the 911 operator exactly where we were, and he, allegedly familiar with the area, couldn't make heads nor tales out of my information. He kept asking me to hurry and find out the address even though I told him Uncle Ed was very dead. Finally R. went and knocked on some neighbors' doors until he rousted out a nice lady who was able to give the address. Assured that a law enforcement officer would be "right out", we settled down to wait. The weather seemed hotter all of a sudden.

Uncle Ed is Dead

Mrs. J. (as I will call the avid neighbor lady) was immediately alert and chatty. We were treated to the information that Uncle Ed's evident demise was the third that had happened to a neighborhood man in a year. The first had been Mrs. J.'s very own husband, from a heart attack. We were informed that he had only been forty-eight, which caused me to look more closely at Mrs. J., who was, I had been sure up until then, at least sixty. Oh, well, the wind and dry air in Texas. Mama had warned me. Obviously the neighborhood historian, Mrs. J. confided that the immediate next door neighbors were not at home, their daughter and her husband having had a big fight and split up, so the neighbors had gone to Tyler to bring her and the grandchildren home, blah, blah, blah. We learned about Uncle Ed and his recently deposed ex-wife, a much juicier version than the prim one we'd got from the aunties. She'd segued into the "real nice memorial garden" that had been dedicated at the church that very morning to the memory of the second neighbor man to expire, whose death had only occurred ten days previously, when she jumped up and made hastily for her dwelling. Ah, brief respite, but only brief, because she came back and informed us she had just called Brother W., who was not Ed's real pastor, that worthy having accepted the call from another church in who-the-hell-knows-or-cares, and gone away, but Brother W., a retired minister who had served the church for thirty years, had agreed to come and fill in, and even though he had been taking a nap, he would be right over.

It was getting very hot, and my head was beginning to hurt very badly.

Finally, after about an hour, the young deputy arrived. He took our "statements" ("We found Uncle Ed dead.") and proceeded to secure the scene. Ron went inside with him through the den doors and came around and let us in. I made to dismiss the kindly neighbor, but ohhhh no! She felt she must remain until Brother W. arrived.

Brother W. was a pleasant surprise. I was expecting Jimmy Swaggart, but Brother W. was so gentle and calm, he might as well

Uncle Ed is Dead

have been a Methodist. To Mrs. J.'s expostulations that the neighborhood was "becoming a place of Death," he gently demurred, and when she averred loudly that "THE LORD" had sent me to find Ed, and I countered warmly that I'd just have to have a little talk with Him about that, as I didn't consider finding corpses one of the Gifts of the Holy Spirit, he just chuckled and winked at me. I got to liking Brother W.

We summoned the aunties, Ed's sisters by phone. They arrived soon after. They were terribly shocked and sad but insisted they had to go and look at him. These are Texas women, tough, if frail. They have lived through the Oil Boom and the Depression, The Big War and rock and roll. They've been widowed, and they don't flinch. What they are not, indeed what few if any of that family are, in my estimation, is capable of making a decision. They all vacillate until it makes me crazy. The issue immediately before the bar was how to get in touch with Ed's children. The local coroner had been called, and the deputy informed us that as soon as he had done his coroner's thing, we would need to have the funeral home come and, ahem! remove the body. Now I have been a sort-of member of that family for thirty-five years, and I have been present for all the funerals, and the same damn funeral home has always done the honors. It did not seem to me to be a hard choice, but ohhh no! They couldn't decide. Maybe the cheeldrun would want that one, but then again, maybe not . . . Picture me, sitting on my hands and chewing my tongue.

Meanwhile, Mrs. J. had gone out and met up with the next door neighbor, fresh from the rescue in Tyler and avid for a new sensational story. As more and more people (not, however, the coroner, upon whom we waited) crowded into the small parlor, the noise level attained disco volume. This had a negative effect on Brother W. and Ron who were trying to get through to someone on the phone who could either provide phone numbers for Ed's cheeldrun or take over and call. Both Brother W. and Ron are fairly deaf, so the chaos reigning around them, as well as the

UNCLE ED IS DEAD

electrical short in the phone wires, predicated futility.

Ron is not the best in this sort of confusion, but Brother W. showed a bit of leadership as he took the floor and hustled the onlookers (avid neighbors) OUT. The dear aunties continued to dither and cry, but they were quiet. Ron was finally able to leave a message with a live person at one of the homes. "Nobody home," he complained. "You just can't leave a message on an answering machine saying, 'Hi, Dennis. Your dad is dead,' you know." Bad old me, I immediately thought of the awful old story that ends: "Your Mom is on the roof."

I was punchy by then from frustration. I have many faults, impatience being one of the most obvious, but by God, I can organize and get things done. Sitting quietly and letting this cloud of incompetence (except for Brother W.) go on around me was hell, but I was doing it as an offering to the poor aunties, who have always been nice to me, rare in that family. I was, I thought, being quiet and non-bull-in-a-china-shop out of respect. After all, it was their brother.

Finally the coroner arrived. He came in a big red tow truck with "Bubba's Towing" emblazoned on the doors. He and Mrs. Bubba had been out for a Sunday fishing trip. Rods extended out the truck windows. The deputy introduced him as "Judge." We greeted him He went directly to work.

Ron's cousins, sons of the aunties, arrived. More indecision and chaos. "The Judge" looked in Ed's medicine cabinet and catalogued his pills. This seemed to be his main task. He was satisfied that the death was from natural causes. ("Looks like the deceased expired from a pre-existing condition," he had averred. Safe bet.) The sun sank lower in the sky. Always a medical groupie, I went in and sat at the table with the coroner and offered to help him. He certainly was not a doctor, but he was the Alpha male present, and I can count pills with the best of them.

The coroner summoned the deputy to him. "Time to call the funeral home," he said.

"I've told 'em, Judge," the deputy replied.

Uncle Ed is Dead

"Goddamit, tell 'em again." Bubba was ready to get back to his fishing.

More dithering. More time passed.

"You seem like you've got a grip," the coroner said to me. "Can't you wade up in there and get 'em to make a Goddamn decision?"

"No," I replied briefly. "I'm just a Goddamn in-law." This he understood.

He lumbered into the parlor and loomed over everyone, even Ronny. "We've got to get him out of here," he intoned. "He ain't gettin' no fresher."

The aunties moaned. Bubba lacked the delicate touch, that was certain.

"But we have to wait for his cheeldrun," someone (family member) said.

"Not here," said the coroner, tersely. "Not him, anyway."

"Well, we always use Crawford—A. Crim," one auntie ventured, "but they might want a different . . ."

"They can move him, then," the coroner roared, "but he's gotta go!"

• • •

We finally got in the road about dark, and I don't think either one of us uttered on the whole way home. We were in shock. The funeral was held two days later. R. returned for it. I did not attend. I felt that I had done my bit for Uncle Ed.

THE MOST FUN YOU CAN HAVE STANDING UP IN A CEMETERY

"Now tell me again: what are we doing?" my ever-patient husband panted as he propelled the loaded wheelbarrow up the hilly driveway in the first light of an April morn. The wheelbarrow contained twenty white wooden stakes, a maul, a can of white spray paint (for touch ups), and a staple gun. I trudged behind totin' a plastic bag full of black ribbon rosettes and numbered 5"x7" white index cards. A schematic of the graveyard with certain graves marked with numbers resided in my jeans pocket.

"We're going to mark the graves for the tableau, honey. I've told you and told you . . ."

"No, Bunny," he insisted. "I know all that. I mean why is this what y'all decided to do for Pilgrimage? "

I'd told him and told him that, too, but I went over it all again as we crested the little hill and entered the old Town Cemetery.

• • •

The three of us stood in the September sunset by our cars parked in the lot of the ante-bellum mansion we were sworn to "maintain and restore." Our plans for the annual Spring

The Most Fun You Can Have

Pilgrimage were going badly. None of the local owners of the town's historic homes (which my husband satirizes as "hewmz") would give us the time of day discussing their opening them to the public. The club to which we all belonged had struggled for lo' these many years to raise money to keep the Old Bank House open and sound. The annual pilgrimage was the chief money-maker. Things looked very bleak. At the meeting we'd just held, no member had been able to enlist any really attractive "hewm," and time was running out. Publicity for the event drove our schedule. We were feeling rather desperate, the club's president, my fellow chairman of the Pilgrimage, and me. It appeared that if some miracle was to be created, it was strictly up to us. The last rays of the setting sun illuminated the old Town Cemetery just to the west of where we stood. Someone said, "If we can't get hous-es, maybe we could do something in the old cemetery." Thus was born the germ of what became "Shades of the Past," our cemetery tableau.

• • •

The idea took off like a house afire once we began to plan. Aided immeasurably by a book complied by a local historian that listed all the marked graves and the inscriptions in the graveyard, I went to work choosing characters. It was a process that redefined itself as I went along. One resource we had in plenitude: hammy would-be actors. The parish had celebrated it sesquicentenary several years previously, and any number of otherwise staid and retiring men were pressed into participating with the excuse of contributing to the civic good. Some of these men were bitten by the drama bug, and they had frock coats (an indispensable costume item.) These males formed the core of our cast. Females were a little bit dicier until our Pilgrimage Costume Mistress (titles were all the compensation any of us could claim) had the brainstorm of decking some of them out in long white nightgowns, these readily available from a variety of retail estab-

The Most Fun You Can Have

lishments. In the beginning, whether or not we could costume the person playing the character was the first consideration, but I also wanted to present a cross-section of the town from its establishment in 1824 through the early part of the twentieth century. We were noted as a town for our educators, lawyers, and eccentrics. It was also important to include the few early residents of historical significance buried under the old cedars: the man who bought the land on which the town was settled. (He made a good investment, but he didn't live long to enjoy his fortune. He was killed within sight of his home—only a few yards north of his gravesite—following an acrimonious card game.) The renowned educator (female) who descended from one of the early prominent settler families and went on to teach at Newcomb College, eventually having a room in the Tulane Student Union named for her. The young founder of a college fraternity who died alone and disinherited in the town's hotel. (His grave site was donated by a local philanthropist.) One of the founders of the short-lived, but well-intentioned, West Florida Republic to which our parish belonged for a few months in 1810 before the United States government put a stern end to that. Civil War casualties. Yellow fever victims (easily portrayed in their nightgowns). Assorted children. My process was happily one of selection. There were an abundance of possibilities.

While I was reconciling my list of would-be "Shades," the Costume Mistress was madly borrowing and sewing. The Publicity Chairman was drafting press releases, and the club members were in a feverish whirl planning the aspects of the rest of the two day event. A scraggly homes tour was stretched by the addition of the venerable Episcopal Church just up a hill from the Old Bank and the cemetery. The rector was pressed into designing a Victorian service of Evening Prayer to end the first day's programme. The Old Bank House itself was being repaired (using spit, bubble gum, and paper clip quality methods, which were all we could afford). Every day brought new challenges, such as when I tried on my own 1840's day dress made from a certified

The Most Fun You Can Have

historic pattern and found there was something terribly wrong with the part of the bodice that went from armpit to raised waist. It looked amazingly like a pocket under my arm. What could it mean? Were women in the 1840's designed that differently? The pattern referred to this piece as an "arm scye," and we had it in upside down. Who knew? After that was fixed, the only complaint I had was that the eight yards of cotton broadcloth in the skirt were some heavy. More dresses followed, all in somber mourning colors.

The press releases worked like a charm. Unbeknownst to us, the idea of doing an historical re-enactment in a cemetery was novel. Area newspapers latched on to the theme, and the nearest big newspaper sent out a photographer to take pictures of us in costume among the headstones. It was about this time that our cast of "Shades" had its first walk-through. On a pleasant day in late February we assembled to find our particular graves and discuss our characters. We had settled on twenty-five as a nice number to present during the three, two-hour tours (one Saturday morning, one Saturday afternoon, one Sunday afternoon.) The logistics of how to conduct the (anticipated) throngs of people through the obstacle course of the five acre cemetery had not yet been worked out. We knew we'd have a printed program giving the names, dates, and scant biographical data of the persons to be portrayed, as well as the names and relationships of portrayers. (An amazing number of descendants had volunteered to "be" their ancestors, probably feeling they could do the parts more justice than strangers). I vaguely envisioned patrons just meandering through the graveyard, stopping at each presenter and hearing the story of each. I was told this approach was too casual, and we three "Mothers of Shades" had to come to some other agreement over who would conduct the groups and how. (This was a thorny issue which we never successfully resolved, even though through the years we tried at least four methods.) We'd discussed the format. The "Shades" would tell their *histoires* without eye contact with the hearers, and there would be no verbal interaction. This was not "living history;" this was dead history. Some of the scripts I'd written, and some were left up to the "Shades" themselves to fashion. Presentations were not to go over a minute in length. The first walk-through went pretty well, but, as all of the characters and "staff" traversed the cemetery from front to rear, we couldn't help but remark the various armadillo holes and uneven ground. Patrons of historical "pilgrimages" are overwhelmingly elderly and female. One more thing to worry about.

In March the article in the newspaper that contained our photographs and brief sketches of some of the characters came out in a Sunday supplement. The three of us ("Mothers of Shades") exulted. What a terrific idea we'd had! How wonderfully successful our Pilgrimage-with-no-hewmz was going to be!

I was sitting at the card table I'd designated my Pilgrimage/Shades desk on the following Tuesday when the phone rang. It was Violet, my co-chairman. "Bad news," she began. Indeed, it was very bad news. In the article, among the other characters I'd described, I'd added a family whose history I'd simply made up. There were three of them, a man and his two children, and they'd perished in one of the yellow fever epidemics that periodically ravaged the state during the 1800's. These particular unfortunates died in the 1853 contagion, right after the town was incorporated and at the height of our civic expansion as a legal/educational/mercantile center. I had no idea who these people were; the name was not one that I recognized, nor did it appear in our local phone book. No one of the local historians I'd consulted knew a scrap of information about them, but, since I was intrigued with the fact of their all dying together, I'd taken the liberty of making up a story to fit the bare facts of their ages and deaths. Since we had so many "worthies" already in our ensemble, I took it upon myself to create a family of poor ne'er-do-wells. It was a fine creative effort, if I do say so, but it had bombed in Baton Rouge because the descendant (female, elderly, wealthy, and not amused) of the remaining child of the family was incensed. Using the contact number listed in the article, she'd called and threatened legal action unless we cleared her ancestors' names publicly. Oh, by the way, the father of the family, far from being a ne'er-do-well, had been the first mayor of our newly-incorporated town. What luck!

The incensed descendant was ultimately placated, but the problems kept coming. The rains of March and early April played havoc with the state of the cemetery's surface, not good at its best and decidedly degraded each time I went back to assess it. The Cemetery Association, nervous as cats about liability, demanded we get a two-day insurance policy to keep them from being the first in line in case one of the Pilgrimage-goers took a header. This would eat up our profit considerably. I obtained "hold harmless" contracts from all of our personnel. We re-wrote the program to include safety instructions. This document was one of the bright spots of the production. A very talented local artist had provided us with pencil sketches of the cedars and tombstones, and we combined these with a front panel that was a black-bordered replica of my great-grandmother's funeral announcement. Our delight in each small success never failed to summon up two more problems, however. The next challenge came when I took yet another crisis call from Violet. One of my teenaged portrayers had turned up pregnant and couldn't fit into her 1840's dress. She was so crushed that I decided to let her continue, changed her part, and put her in a nightgown to be a woman from 1880 who died while pregnant. She was delighted, but her mother, already reeling from the horror of finding out that her straight-A student sixteen year old was pregnant without benefit of clergy, tore into me at a meeting and threatened all sorts of hell if I didn't refuse to include the girl. I left it up to them entirely, figuring I'd changed the printed proof of our program so many times as it was that I doubted the printer could ever get it right. Two days before the event, the girl went into labor and lost the baby, so we drew a line through her character's listing on five hundred programs. The night before the event, the descendant of the first

The Most Fun You Can Have

mayor called me to announce that she'd been thinking, and she didn't want her ancestral characters included after all, no matter how laudatory our portrayal. I was too tired to even argue.

So seven the next morning found me bleary-eyed and exhausted from red-lining the five hundred programs yet again into the wee hours, but I had promises to keep and twenty stakes to get in place before ten. My ever-faithful husband might not understand what we were doing, but I knew all too well.

The actual tableaus were greatly successful. We got the presentation and the attendant drama just right as we had hoped to do. Led by one of our cast who played dirges on his harmonica, we left the hallowed portals of the Old Bank House and processed down the street a few hundred yards to the cemetery. Crowds of onlookers, curious as to what a cemetery tableau could be, lined the streets as we walked, heads down, in our somber costumes. We were an interesting collection: a mother and infant, assorted frock-coated men, women in black or gray or lavender dresses of 1840 or 1880 or 1910—or in heavy cotton nightgowns, children in homespun trousers and smock-like blouses or nightgowns, some with tattered dolls or toy guns. It was impressive. We entered through the cemetery's wrought iron gates and went silently to our respective places. Keeping our eyes warily on the ground, we avoided most of the various hazards.

I got lost. Maybe it was just that I was so tired, but panic set in when I topped the hill and couldn't find the modest obelisk that marked "my" grave, the resting place of my mother's maternal grandmother. Thank a merciful Providence for one of the other "Shades" who, seeing my hesitation, eased up to me and pointed subtly until I got my bearings. I took my place, clasping both hands on the top of Great-grandmother's marker for dear life and waited until a small crowd gathered to begin. I'd planned what I wanted to say but hadn't memorized the speech. As I clasped Grandma Jane's grave marker, the words just seemed to flow.

The Most Fun You Can Have

• • •

"I am Eliza Jane Winter Norwood Currie. I was born in 1818 in this parish. My parents were first generation Americans. My father came from Ireland, and my mother came from England. They settled on the east coast of this country around the time of the Revolution. They sought land and opportunity and moved here from North Carolina at the turn of the 19th century settling on our plantation, which they named 'Oaklawn.' My sisters and I had a happy childhood. We were educated at home by teachers my father and others of his friends engaged. I married for the first time at sixteen to Lemuel Norwood, the son of a neighboring plantation owner. It was a brilliant match, everyone said, the merging of two distinguished families. I truly loved him and believed we would be happy. Babies came almost immediately, but they all died, all but one. In twelve years I bore eight babies, but only my son George lived. Lemuel became ill almost immediately after we married. His father gave us a fine plantation, but he was unable to run it. So, in between having babies that didn't live, I ran the place, assisted by our slave overseer. Lemuel died at thirty. I remarried—an older man, a widower. I thought he would take the burden of running the plantation off of my shoulders, but he proved to be a poor manager. He was, however, an excellent procreator. When he moved to my home he brought with him three children by his first wife, and he kept me pregnant from the first month of our marriage. His rather unpleasant sister was heard to remark that all it took to get me in the family way was for a man to hang his pants over the bedstead and that I was a poor unfortunate who, in all the years I was married, "never saw her feet." I did have ten pregnancies with Alexander. Of these, only two boys survived. Then Alexander died of dropsy, and, once again I was alone to fend for myself—and the three boys. Alexander's sister took the three daughters by his first marriage. I was glad to be relieved of them. We managed, despite the War, despite sicknesses and failed crops and the fire that destroyed

The Most Fun You Can Have

the Big House. They all were educated, and all grew into decent men. Our fortune did not endure, but we endured. I died aged eighty-four, two years into the new century, and here I lie, at rest at last."

I was pleased with what had emerged as I recited, but also surprised because it was not mine at all. It just came out of my mouth. Of all the things I'd read or been told about Grandma Jane, her endless and tragic pregnancies and being heavily laden with responsibilities and cares were not the traits or circumstances emphasized. Mama had admired her as an independent woman who managed "the farm" with aplomb. My grandmother had thought her something of a rebel because she was an intrepid horsewoman who rode astride, even up into her seventies. Where did I get the theme for my speech? I was forced to conclude it came from Jane herself, somehow. I was not the only Shade to report this phenomenon. Many others recalled getting newly formed inspiration as they began to speak. It was odd, but we never doubted what we felt.

The people came and came and came. I have no idea how many times I told the same story. Peeping out of the corner of

The Most Fun You Can Have

my eye, I even saw familiar faces toward the end, repeat listeners. At precisely noon, our harmonica player, who'd been playing softly and strolling the cemetery throughout the tableaus' presentations, began "Onward Christian Soldiers," our sign to form up to march out. The onlookers parted, hushed and respectful, as we returned to the house.

All our "Shades" were jubilant when, front door firmly closed behind the last to enter, we were able to be "ourselves" again. Everyone had tales to tell. (This was when we first admitted to the peculiar influences we'd received when we began to recite.) "They loved it!" was said again and again. It was difficult for us to part company and go away, but I was adamant. This was just our first of three "performances" I reminded them and admonished them to get some food and rest before our next set. "And be here on time!" were the last words out of my mouth.

Of course, when the time to begin the next round came, fully a quarter of the portrayers were not to be found. Frantic conference. Should we go on, on time? Should we wait, and, if so, how long? Should we kill the offenders straight-away or wait until after the last presentation? The miscreants showed up less than fifteen minutes later, and we began our second march down to the graveyard. The mood was not as felicitous. For one thing, it was much warmer. April in Louisiana is tricky, and the afternoon temperature could have been in the high 60's or low 70's. It was surely 80 degrees as we processed, and the voluminous skirts we ladies were wearing—had been wearing for hours—got heavier with every step. Frank drops of sweat were seen on feminine as well as masculine brows. The crowds were just as large, however. This gave us grit to endure, at least until we got into the fire ants. The little creatures were surely in residence when we'd tramped around that morning, but we hadn't seen any hills earlier. With the heating of the day, the ants had roused and gotten busy building. Numerous long, full skirts brushing across the mounds stirred up the ants, and they attacked. Soon, all "Shades" were doing unseemly hopping and swatting maneuvers. We managed,

The Most Fun You Can Have

by the hardest, to regain composure enough to get into our roles and do our stuff, but fire ant bites, untreated, hurt like hell, and most of us received a number of them. We were forced to end the second set of "Shades" early, even omitting the singing that was supposed to take place around the Confederate monument as the sun went down. It was just as well, because the sun stayed pretty high throughout the event. We could add sunburn to our list of other on-the-job injuries.

After emergency treatment with aloe and toothpaste, most of the portrayers attended the Evening Prayer service at the Episcopal Church, then went home to soak, rest, and whine. The three "Mothers of Shades," however, could not rest. We sat up into the night critiquing the performances and trying to head off trouble for the next day's set, the last, thank God. Fire ant killer ("Get the very best. Damn the cost.") was obtained and applied by staff (husbands.) First-aid kits were assembled. At the crack of dawn, I made an inspection and staked out the worst armadillo burrows and pits to be filled in. (More staff.) We had been far too lucky on the first day. Only the re-enactors had suffered injuries, and those were very minor. It was well to be prepared. I'd gotten very little sleep, and my stomach, usually steel-lined, was flipping and flopping. When we lined up to do the final procession, I looked like a woman who'd lived a hard life, and I surely felt like one. This was method acting, but I hadn't planned it so.

Alert to the dangers under our feet, we trod warily, and no more bites were suffered. We'd worked out the kinks of our presentations in the two previous sessions, so we were pretty smooth with delivery. The crowds were not as large as on the previous day, but they were very attentive and seemed to be enjoying our stories. As the afternoon wore on, I forgot to be nervous and was able to listen to the snatches of dialogue rising from the "Shades" nearby.

". . . My epitaph says it all. 'Remember friend, as you pass by, as you are now so once was I. As I am now, you soon will be.

The Most Fun You Can Have

Prepare, my friend, for Eternity.'" (Scion of pioneer family, prominent lawyer, killed in the explosion of a steamboat.)

And:
". . . One day I had a terrible headache, and Ma-Ma and Pa-Pa tried every way they knew to relieve it, even sending into town for ice to cool my brow, but it was no use. The angels came, and I went with them. I was buried in my favorite white dress. Isn't it pretty?" (Pampered only daughter of a wealthy family, died of meningitis c.1880)

And:
". . . I tried to be strong and survive for the sake of my three little children, but when my husband came and told me that they were all taken, even my joy, my precious daughter, I turned my head to the wall and gave my soul to Heaven." (Mother of three small children. All died of yellow fever on the same day in 1853.)

And:
"I founded this town, and I was the first to lie in this cemetery. My legacy is all around me." (Our first female businesswoman, founder of our town.)

And:
"We moved here from Canada in the 1820's. My sister founded a school for young ladies, and I married one of her pupils, the pretty daughter of the town's leading citizen. I was prospering as a merchant when I took that ship to Galvez-town . . ." (Young businessman, drowned as he tried to save others in a shipwreck off the Texas coast.)

All the voices combined to weave a tapestry in my mind. Our town shared in these lives then, and we continued to be a part of them—and they of us. It was another layer of being that we felt all around us. The Prayer Book calls it "the Communion of

The Most Fun You Can Have

Saints." It was very real in that place that day, as real as the fire ants and the kids playing basketball across the road behind the cemetery.

At the end of the tableau we sang old hymns, ending with my funereal favorite, "Abide With Me." We processed for the last time back to the house in a sort of trance. We'd hoped the cemetery tableau would move the tourists. It moved them—and us.

Still, it does not do to dwell too heavily on the momentous aspects of what we did. We had a whole lot of fun, ant attacks and all, notwithstanding. Each and every "Shade" had a tale to tell, and some of them were just plain hilarious. The most notable happened to the woman who portrayed the Newcomb professor. A distinguished educator in her own right and an imposing figure, she was one of the stars of our little production. She'd researched her role carefully, interviewing people who actually remembered her character. Her presentation was flawless, much commented upon. As she was in full spate early in the first set, she noticed this elderly woman looking at her with great consternation. The woman came back for the second set and the third. Our portrayer was somewhat spooked, being the focal point of such concentrated scrutiny, but the woman looked frail, and she didn't appear hostile, just puzzled. When the last set was finished and all of us were gathering to sing, she finally approached our "Miss Imogene" re-enactor, and, in a very hesitant voice, said, "Miss Imogene, I don't suppose you remember me, but you taught me at Newcomb in 19-." Our "Shade" said it was all she could do not to shriek with laughter. We all took it for high praise, even if it was decidedly weird.

"Shades of the Past" was presented many more times, and I still claim the concept's copyright, even though it's been copied and presented elsewhere. I don't mind that at all. It should be presented all over because it is a wonderful way to have people of today get in touch with the people who went before. The universality of themes we uncovered in our research for "Shades" convinced us that times change, but people are pretty much the

The Most Fun You Can Have

same now as centuries ago. One thing for certain: as the descendant who portrayed his lawyer ancestor said, "as they are now, we, too, shall be." Our stories will blend into the tapestry just as did the ones we unearthed for our tableau, and on and on. Rather than being depressing or lugubrious, our presentation was—dare I say it? fun. We all dined out on our experiences for months, and we'd all do it again. It made a little money, and it made local history. Not bad for scratch improvisation.

And that's what we were doing in the cemetery.

As this book was going to press, our faithful and beloved harmonica player Henry Howard "Mickey" Forrester, junior, died, all too young. This is for Mickey, with love.

NIL NISI:
THE ART OF THE EULOGY

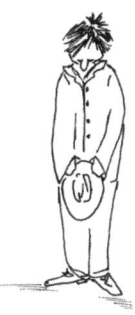

My kindergarten teacher died, full of years and honors. It is difficult to overstate the effect she had upon the lucky children who were privileged to learn from her. Her tutelage—in early childhood education, piano, voice, and band—was not in the public school system, and, therefore, her pupils were from families who—at the very least—were willing (nay, anxious) to pay her modest stipends. This certainly culled the cast of characters who availed themselves of her programs, but, on the other hand, her sphere of influence comprised many of the children of my little town, Caucasian sub-group, over a period of many years. I was a double-dipper, having been an alumnus of Harmony Hill Kindergarten and of a brief, if undistinguished, regimen of piano lessons. Although I was terminally lazy about music, I did love to play at playing it, and my record in kindergarten was good, so she approved of me, but she was not blind to my deficits. Still, as I grew up and older, she and I maintained a warm relationship. For many years she was the church organist for the Episcopal church, which I attend, and she'd also been one of the leading lights in the Episcopal Sunday School (which I vastly preferred to the Methodist one I also attended) so my contact with her was ongoing. She always spoke well of me, and this was in no small part one of the reasons I kept up a certain irregular closeness. It is not

Nil Nisi

all that often that I get an old teacher's good report.

She continued to live in her own home right up until the last. I visited her sometimes, usually on her birthday, or around then, and I kept up with her through her elder daughter, a pediatric oncologist of national renown with whom I've been privileged to work from time to time. Her sight and hearing eventually failed, and she was bedridden, but her spirit and melodious voice were strong to the end. When she died, I wanted to perform some service to honor the enormous debt I, and many of my contemporaries, owed to her. I began by relaying a request (read: demand) that she'd made to a friend of mine when the friend had last visited. This involved another friend's being drafted to play the "Largo" from Dvorak's *Symphony to the New World* at her funeral. This was one of our teacher's favorites. She had played it at my own father's funeral and at many others. The appointed pianist, one of my classmates and life-long friends, was a particularly gifted former pupil who had gone on to prominence as a nationally cited early childhood education specialist, following in our mentor's example in music and teaching. Gentle and sentimental, this individual did not thank me for putting her on the spot. "I don't think I can do it," she wailed. "I'll probably break down. I'm shaking just thinking about it."

"You have to do it, Lois," I rejoined. "Mrs. Lytle told Julia Ann and HenriEtta the last time they went to see her. It's just like a deathbed confession. You have to believe it." (I have never been retiring or hesitant to lay down the law, which is one reason why I am so beloved.) Poor Lois. She muttered something and hung up and rushed to find the music to the damned thing.

• • •

Having given my dear old friend a heads up, I then called Mrs. L's daughter. Julia Ann had already spoken to her. I expressed my sincere sympathy and offered to do "any thing that would help," even to the point of "saying a few words" at Lytle's funer-

Nil Nisi

al. (I envisioned the sort of service where three or five devoted friends each stood and gave brief remembrances.) Imagine my chagrin when I was taken up on my offer, it developed that I was to do THE EULOGY.

The egregious eulogy has long been a pet peeve of mine. I have heard my share. There are two main types of spoken homilies that one encounters at funerals. These are the ones delivered by the clergy and the ones delivered by family or friends. Neither can be guaranteed to be palatable.

Too many clergy, in my opinion, weigh too heavily on the purely religious theme of the eulogy, "preach the funeral," in other words. This type of approach depersonalizes the deceased. A few throw-away remarks may be inserted to give lip service to the value and history of the one being "funeralized," but the focus is on religion, high or low, not on the person, not at all. I have known both Episcopal and evangelical clergy to err in this regard. At the funeral of one of my aunts in the premier Episcopal church in Baton Rouge—which she had attended for over fifty years and supported by word, deed, and cash—her name was only mentioned the requisite few times the liturgy commands, and no personal remarks were ventured. It is epitomized by the service performed for the parent of a dear friend who had, tragically, killed himself. The family, shocked and stunned, implored the preacher—who was unknown to the deceased and barely known to the family—not to allude to the suicide. He didn't allude. He put it right out there, using the occasion to preach his theology about despair. It bothered me tremendously because it was exploitative. At such times, surely the comfort of those left behind should outweigh the chance to proselytize.

An especially ugly variant of the depersonalized eulogy is encountered when the deceased has fallen away from religion, been homebound and non-observant, or when the clergy person officiating for some reason hasn't had the pleasure of the deceased's acquaintance. Therefore, I issue my absolute *ukase* on the subject. If I ruled the universe, any eulogist of any calling who

Nil Nisi

prefaced a eulogy with the phrase "I did not know (the deceased), but . . ." would instantly be struck dumb forever. This eventuality, more common today, perhaps, than previously, can be gently covered by the use of a device such as the following which a kind and enlightened clergyman (I am proud to say he was an Episcopal priest) used just recently when an honored and revered elder of our small congregation passed on. She'd been home bound for a long time, and her church participation, fervent and regular in the days of her good health, had declined to zero. Our own priest was ill and unable to officiate, so a priest from a neighboring parish came. Without making a big deal out of the circumstances, he disposed of his lack of personal relationship with the departed by saying, by way of preface, "I am told Mrs. H. was . . ." We all breathed a sigh of gratitude at the graceful tactic. Contrast this with the mean spirited, "I did not know your mother. She never came to church," that I heard preached to a devastated family of four sisters who, having lost their father when they were very little, went on to lose their mother, their rock, in an automobile accident when they were but teenagers. Take it out on the grief-stricken, why don't you? Is humiliation a righteous tool for conversion? I think not.

The opposite, and nearly as offensive, style of eulogy is the too personal, characterized by the use of pet names ("Moo-maw," "Dog Tick," and "Tee-Rat" are just a few from the obituary columns I've noted recently. The list is endless) too-intimate anecdotes (Do we need to hear how Aunt Weesie always hummed hymns as she cooked Pee-paw's dinners—or worse?) and embarrassing expressions of extreme bereavement. Funerals are religious services. Just as the deceased can get overlooked in a "preached" funeral, so can the faith get obliterated when grief outweighs good taste.

Mama (ever my guide in matters funereal) was hardly a devout or observant Christian, but she firmly believed that an excess of grief was contrary to our faith in God, Jesus, and the promise of Heaven, and was, therefore, anathema. In Judaism, this is usually

Nil Nisi

not a problem. The few Jewish funerals I have attended have been models of good taste and strong consonance with their faith. (As an aside, one of the absolute all-time great homilies/eulogies was given by a rabbi for the grandfather of a friend. He used as his text Micah 6:8, ". . .what does the Lord require of you but to do justice, and to love mercy, and to walk humbly with your God?" The deceased had passed muster. 'Nuff said.) All it takes is balance, and brevity is also nice.

So here I was, under the pressure not only of obligation but also of my own prejudices and beliefs, the eulogist for a lady who, in our small sphere, at least, had affected many lives. She was not all fuzzy and pure. She had an acerbic tongue and was not shy about correcting us, not even in her advanced age. (She'd drilled Julia Ann in the proper method of curtsying on that last visit, and Julia Ann had not received a passing grade. Imagine flunking curtsying at age fifty.) The first thing I had to do was get a comprehensive mental picture of how I wanted to portray Lytle, and from that all else flowed that accounted for the design of the eulogy. The delivery was something else.

We sat in the back of the little church, Lois, and Mark, and Bobby, and I, all former pupils of Mrs. Lytle. We were transported back forty years to our kindergarten days. We fretted. We giggled. We quivered, at least Lois and I quivered, because we were "on the program." As we sat there, a flood of impressions of all that Lytle had instilled in me, exposed me to, expected of me bathed me in a spirit of gratitude. Because of her, I knew how to stand up and approach the lectern when it was my time to speak. When she prepared us for recitals, she brooked no excuses of stage fright. Because of her strong Anglican demeanor, I knew the proper posture to assume when participating in a religious service, the bowed head, the clasped hands, the bow to the altar. I knew to speak up, speak slowly, speak confidently. Hell, I could even have curtsied adequately if that had been required. So, when I faced the little congregation I was able to choke back tears and tell them why Lytle was so special, what were her unique qualities,

Nil Nisi

and, most of all, why she was such an important figure in the lives of a troop of young people. I was even able to speak to her deep and sincere faith in God and her imparting that to us. The very gifts Lytle gave to me were the ones I used to eulogize her. It was fitting.

After the funeral, her daughters were kind enough to approve of the eulogy. I would literally have wept had they not been, but, as it was, I wept anyway. Lois and Mark and I exchanged even more reminiscences before parting. She'd been such a stalwart foundation to us, but she was gone. Her memory would live on in all of us who revered her, but her voice would be heard no more on earth. A eulogy is no more nor less than a goodbye. It should be short, sweet, and hold the hope of an eventual reunion. More no eulogist can do.

DANCE ME DOWN EASY

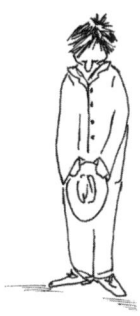

Wilhelmina Boettinger was one of those supremely unfortunate people who developed true Alzheimer's in her forties. Prior to becoming symptomatic with early onset dementia, she lived a rich, full life as the younger daughter of a prominent New Orleans banker and his aristocratic wife. Both parents had pedigrees going back to the early nineteenth century in the City, and the ranks of both families abounded with members of the courts of Comus/Momus/Rex. Mina served as maid of Comus in her turn, as had her elder sister Isabella, called "Issy" in the family and by close friends. The two women had had a brother, Robert Livingston III, but he'd died in a freak accident while in college. Mina had been especially close to him, and her nerves were fragile after his death. None-the-less, she'd been courted and married by the scion of yet another old Crescent City family, but the marriage lasted less than a year, and, by the time the dementia struck, Mina was pretty much reconciled to life in her mother's home (Daddy having died in his early sixties) as her mother's companion. It was not a bad life. There was plenty of money. She and her mother got along famously, traveled together all over the world, and rarely disagreed. Mina lived in her own apartment in the enormous Garden District home the Boettingers first inhabited in 1882. She loved cats and had any number, mostly strays she'd adopted from the pound or picked up on the street. She did some charitable work, was a sustaining member of the Junior League and a member of the Orléans Club, but her other passion was the ballet. As a young girl she'd studied with a real ballerina, and her girlhood dream was to dance in a real *corps de ballet*, but various factors—her social position, her size (She was almost six feet tall at thirteen, and weighed 150 pounds. As the years rolled by she dieted assiduously, but she never was able to acquire thinness) and, most of all, her actual lack of talent—kept her from realizing her goal. She became, instead, a balletomane, supporting the various ballet theatres in the City and traveling to the cultural centers of the planet to see ballets performed. In fact, she even choreographed a ballet, based somewhat derivatively on cats and their secret lives, and she was trying to persuade one or the other of her local ballet companies to produce it when the first awful symptoms of her dementia presented.

Because Mina had been emotionally fragile, off and on, and for many years, it took Issy and Mrs. Boettinger a good while to face up to the fact that something was really very wrong and getting worse. Mina got lost coming home from her club, from the grocery store, from the pound. She began to wake up at night and cry piteously because she neither knew where nor who she was. A consultation with the family's kindly doctor led to a sickening round of further doctor visits with the end result of a diagnosis of Alzheimer's. Issy and Mrs. Boettinger tried at first to keep the awful truth from Mina, but Mina was savvy enough to know that she was rapidly losing her mind. In the time honored tradition of Southern aristocratic families, instead of pouring out her fears to her mother and sister, she sought out the family's Black housekeeper, a loyal and loving member of the household since Mina had come home a divorced woman, twenty-odd years before. The two cried and prayed in the kitchen until poor Mina was worn out and mostly forgot what they'd been talking about. The housekeeper, whose name was, appropriately, Mercy Jackson, spoke with Mrs. Boettinger, and the result was a brief period of candor and relief between the family members. Mina was coherent enough to make a will leaving her considerable estate to a cat shelter and two ballet companies before the long gray fog closed over her.

One very hot day in the last summer of her life, Mina sat with Issy out under the pergola that abutted their pool. Both sisters were avid and skillful swimmers, and spent many hours there. Although the topic of permanently covering the pool had arisen between Issy and her mother often recently for fear of Mina's falling in and drowning, it was always deferred. In the way of families coping with dementia, they struggled with the decision until Mercy, overhearing them, interjected, "What difference does it make how Mina dies, Mrs. B.? She loves to get in the pool, and it calms her when she's agitated."

"That's true, Mama," Issy concurred. "We forget she's dying no matter what we do." So the pool stayed, and, on this particular very hot day, after a swim, Mina seemed to have one of those flashes of clarity that characterize the disorder.

"Issy," she began, "you've been the best big sister anyone could ever have." (Hearing this Issy feared that Mina was adopting the childish manner of speech and behavior to which she usually regressed at those times when she could make coherent statements at all, but this was not the case.) "Time feels very short for me, " she continued, waving her hand to shush her sister's objections. "Let me finish. Who knows how many other times I can think of this . . ." and she trailed off.

"That's it," thought Issy, with a certain amount of relief, but Mina regained the wisp of her thought and spoke again.

"I want you to promise me some things," Mina said, her voice breaking. "You know we've lived charmed lives, even with Robbie and Daddy dying. We've always been a truly close family, and we never had the conflicts other people had. We got along, even as little children, and Mama never fussed at us and belittled us like some of our friends' mothers did, you remember?"

And Issy did remember. Mama and Daddy had accepted hers

Dance Me Down Easy

and Mina's choices of friends and husbands (Issy had had three so far) and lives. The recrimination heard on visits to other peoples' homes was utterly absent from their own. A wave of grace and gratitude swept over Issy, and it was all she could do to mutely nod, but she did reach out and grasp Mina's hand. It was very cool and dry, even though Issy, herself, was sweating copiously.

"So I want to ask you to do some things for me. Now. While I can still make sense. Will you do them, Issy? Will you promise?"

And of course, Issy solemnly swore. So the various cats and kittens were gradually relocated into very good homes that Issy and Mercy and their friends found, and money was put in an account to pay for their care and spaying or neutering when the kittens came of age. The relocation was done, as Mina had wanted, out of her sight, and, whenever cats and kittens left the Boettinger house, their stuffed cat look-alikes appeared on Mina's bed. Mina was mostly confined to her rooms by this time, as the summer turned slowly to autumn. She no longer went out socially, not even to church. The priest came to her bringing Holy Communion. Unable to attend the ballet performances that she so loved, she watched videotapes of as many ballets as Issy could obtain. The music boxes she'd collected from her girlhood that featured twirling ballerinas were wound and rewound. She performed these repetitive actions herself, cocking her head and waving her arms in time to the tunes, then rewinding the movement again, interminably. Sometimes she would dance to music only she could hear.

There is never any tragedy so grim and unrelieved that at least one funny episode doesn't occur. The Boettinger pool and tennis courts ran along a side street bordering the mansion and its grounds. The men who rode the garbage truck were fond of Mina, who often sat by the pool just beyond the fence that separated the yard from the street. In the manner ingrained in her since she was a tiny child, she was mindful of other peoples' comfort, and the garbage men were always sweaty and uncomfortable in the hot weather (and it is almost always hot in New Orleans.)

Dance Me Down Easy

Her mother stocked Coca-Colas in a refrigerator under the shade of an overhang, and Mina took to giving out Cokes to the garbage men whenever they passed. This got to be a regular event, enjoyed by all parties, until one day the Cokes ran out. There were, however, two dozen bottles of Dom Pérignon champagne in the 'fridge, and Mina presented these to the three astonished garbage men, all twenty-four of them.

"Mama never seriously considered putting Mina in a home," Issy would say afterward, "except that one time with the Dom Pérignon."

Indeed, one of the promises Issy made to Mina that day by the pool was that she would be able to die in her own rose-colored room, surrounded by the things she loved. It was an inviolable vow. Issy knew the difficulties that might arise, but she promised.

• • •

Throughout the autumn Mina held her own. Some days she would attempt to feed herself or chat; most days she required the help of one of the four attendants Mrs. Boettinger hired. There were Callie and Josie, sisters who were certified nursing assistants, and Chloe and Doris, nieces of Mercy's sister-in-law. By paying premium wages, Mrs. Boettinger was able to obtain excellent help, and all of the caregivers were reliable and quickly became devoted to Mina and her family. Issy often remarked that there was surely a lot to be said for having "adequate funds," and the family knew how really fortunate they were compared to so many others. Still, no life with an enduring sorrow, however well cushioned, is easy. Issy came to the house every day, but she cried every night, too. Alone, no current male interest in sight, she felt the loss of her closest confidante very keenly. Mrs. Boettinger tried her best to participate in her daughter's care, but she was rising seventy-eight, and she suffered herself from heart trouble and arthritis, so her abilities were limited. "The Girls," as she collectively referred to the attendants, wound up taking care of her, too, much of the time. (Issy, more aware of political correctness than her mother, tentatively asked Callie whether her mother was being offensive and insensitive by referring to them in that manner. Callie looked at Issy for a long moment and replied levelly, "Your Mama got more to worry about than political correctness, Issy," so no more was ever said about it, and "The Girls" they remained.)

When December arrived, and the days grew shorter and darker, Mina began to fail. Issy's big fear during this time was that Mina would die on Christmas, or, failing that, New Year's Day. She insisted they decorate the house as elaborately as always for Christmas. Many friends came to call, and the closest were solemnly taken up to Mina's apartment to say what amounted to a goodbye to her, although she rarely noticed that anyone was even in the room. She ate very little, although Chloe could usually persuade her to take a bit more than the others could. Chloe got in the habit of dashing in every day at meal times to feed Mina, whether she was scheduled to work or not. The Girls got Mina up every day. They brushed her hair and tied a ribbon around it to get it off her face because one of her repetitive motions was to wipe her face as if something was making it itch. She would sit in one of the Victorian chairs with her feet on a footstool most of the time. Some days she would reach for one of the stuffed cats and, holding it, absently pet it. Christmas and New Year's Day passed without incident.

Carnival was early that year. Mrs. Boettinger was, in the long ago days of her youth, Queen of the Twelfth Night Revelers, and she never missed their ball. The Girls were doing such a good job of minding Mina that it seemed permissible for both Mrs. Boettinger and Issy to attend other balls as well, and luncheons, and other social events. It was still cold on Ash Wednesday when, at Issy's insistence, Mrs. Boettinger boarded a plane at Moisant to take a quick five day trip to visit an old friend in Palm Beach. "Mama," Issy told her, "life has to go on somehow. We can't know when Mina will die. You haven't been out of New Orleans

Dance Me Down Easy

for over a year. Go." So Mrs. Boettinger went.

On the first Friday in Lent, Issy ran into an old friend in Saks. He'd been her beau thirty-five years before when she was a schoolgirl at Sacred Heart, but his family had been moved to the Middle East, and, naturally, they'd lost track of each other. Both had been married, and both were now unattached. They went for coffee. Issy found herself confiding to him about Mina, and, to her mortification, she began to weep right out in public. It developed that he'd lost his father to Alzheimer's just the past summer. He understood. He took Issy home, and, in the way modern relationships progress, he wound up spending the night. Issy was in a state that could only be described as euphoric. When the telephone rang at ten the next morning, she answered it with such a joyful voice that Chloe (who was on the other end) thought she'd gotten the wrong number, hung up, and dialed again.

When they sorted out the misunderstanding, Issy gave permission for Chloe to take Mina home with her to stay for the rest of the weekend. The Girls had done this before for short periods since Mina had gotten so bad. Formerly, she would become very agitated when she was taken to a strange place, but by this time she barely registered where she was. Doris, the scheduled weekend sitter, had a sick child at home, and Chloe was filling in, but she, too, had obligations . . . Issy saw no harm in Mina's going home with Chloe and so, gave her blessing.

Issy and Rémy spent the entire day together, but, in the evening he had a social event which she could not attend, so they parted at six. He called her from his car, just to bill and coo, and, when the phone rang right after he'd hung up, she answered it gaily, but it was not he. It was Callie calling from Chloe's house, telling her that Mina had died.

The Flight of the Holy Family into Egypt was a walk in the park compared to Issy's flight downtown to the neighborhood where Chloe lived. It was Saturday night, clear and cold, and the knife and gun club members were out on street corners and in front of bars. Issy was rarely afraid anywhere in her native city, but she was not unaware of racial and class tensions as she drove her Lexus down Claiborne Avenue. She was prepared for taunts and verbal assaults, and these were forthcoming, but she reached Chloe's bungalow without major incident. Callie's ancient land whale of a Buick was parked in the driveway. Chloe, Callie, and Josie awaited her at the front door. They took her into Chloe's guest room where, arranged with closed eyes and folded hands, Mina lay lifeless on the prim single bed.

"She was fine, Issy, I swear," Chloe began, but Issy raised her hand to shush her.

"Chloe," she said, "I know Mina was as safe with you as she would have been with me, so let's not have any recriminations." She went into the living room, leading the others. She sat heavily on the sofa and motioned Chloe down next to her. "Now just tell me," she ordered.

Mina had been fine at first. Chloe got her to eat some scrambled eggs and grits, and the two women were sitting in front of Chloe's big screen TV watching Lawrence Welk reruns when a dancing couple came on the screen. The man twirled the lady, and she pirouetted away from him so that she was the only person in the frame.

"That's when Miss Mina tried to get up," Chloe said. "She raised up as much as she could, and she reached her arms out to the TV, and she made some kind of noise. I swear, Issy, it almost sounded like she said her own name. I know she wasn't talking anymore, but it sounded like she said , 'Mina,' or maybe it was just, 'me,' but she said it real loud. Then she just slumped back and died."

Issy put her arms around Chloe, and they both cried a good spell. Callie and Josie were crying, too, but then practical Callie said, "OK, that's enough. Now we've got to figure out where we go from here." This shocked Issy into realizing that by Mina's having died at Chloe's house, many complications had been introduced. Instead of calling dear, old Dr. Fauver, they should call 911 and get the police and a coroner.

Dance Me Down Easy

"I know the EMT's won't take a dead body anywhere," said Issy, amazed she had that factoid at her disposal.

"Sho' won't," concurred Josie. "Got to get the police involved, and God knows how long it'll take them to come down here on a Sat'day night."

"Lord, I never thought of that!" Issy said, with feeling. "And I guess the police would want to take the body to the morgue . . ."

"You bet," said Callie. "Unexplained death in an African-American's home of a white woman. Not good. Not good at all."

"Damn!" exclaimed Issy. "Y'all give me a minute. Let me think."

If the Three Stooges or the Marx Brothers had been orchestrating the removal of Mina's body from Chloe's home to her own, it would not have been any more comical. Mina, never spindly in health, had managed to maintain most of her weight during her protracted illness, mainly due to inactivity. Dead weight, she was not easy to maneuver out of the guest room, down the steps of Chloe's house and out to the Buick, and, although the women involved in the transfer were trained at handling helpless patients, they were not trained in keeping a straight face. It didn't help at all that just a few houses down, on the corner, was Bull's Bar, and its denizens were gathered outside watching as the little procession assisted Mina into the car.

"Hey, Baby," one man shouted, "need some help with that chick? I got just the thing to wake her up!"

"I doubt it," Issy muttered grimly.

Mrs. Boettinger returned home the next afternoon and was met at Moisant by close friends who, gently, told her that Mina had died peacefully the evening before. She was grief-stricken, of course, and she said the expected thing, how bad she felt that she'd not been by Mina's side at the end, but the friends assured her that she could have done nothing. They told her what Issy'd told them, that Mina died at home in her rose-pink bedroom, surrounded by her stuffed cats and ballet music boxes, and, indeed, that was the picture Mrs. Boettinger saw when she got home. Mina was laid out on her bed, looking as peaceful and placid as she'd done as a young woman. It was a comforting and consoling sight.

Luckily, Mrs. Boettinger was never to ever be told of the midnight flight from Mid-town that returned Mina to home turf. With the giddiness that hysteria produces, Chloe and Callie and Issy had piled into the two cars, Callie driving her Buick and Chloe driving Issy's Lexus, and made their way uptown. As is often the case, because they hoped not to, they caught every red light on the way. At one, the Lexus, in the lead, was parked directly across from a car containing two of New Orleans' finest, and the duo of Chloe and Issy evoked curious stares. Hardly daring to breathe and keeping eyes front as best they could, the two women were saved when the light turned green, and they gently pulled away.

"All I can say is, 'Thank God they weren't stopped across from the other car,'" said Issy.

"Not to worry," replied Chloe. "Callie's Buick's got tinted windows. Everybody looks dark through them."

After the crew arrived at the Boettinger home, it was a relative piece of cake to haul the body up two flights of wide sweeping stairs and then along the hall to Mina's very own apartment. They, joined by Doris and Josie, prepared the body, dressed Mina in her favorite rose peignoir, and called Dr. Fauver. Then they sat with Mina all night and the next day until her Mama could come home.

After a decent interval with Mina, Mrs. Boettinger rose and directed Issy to call the funeral directors, and, shortly thereafter, Mina took another trip to the House of Bultman. When she was gone, everyone retired for a well-deserved sleep, but, early the next morning, Issy went back to Mina's room and wound up the music boxes, one at a time, and listened until the last note was gone and the tiny dancers had twirled for the last time. Holding one of the stuffed cats, she whispered, "Mina, I kept all the promises," as she turned out the lights and left the room.

Family Plot

I got this letter the other week. That in itself is a story because nobody writes anymore—anything but. However, I have one friend who is a traditionalist. He lives up in North Louisiana and is his family's historian. They are distinguished, and they still have some money, which distinguishes his distinguished family from my distinguished family, but he treats me like it doesn't matter, which is very Old South-gentlemanly. He has enough humor not to take himself too seriously, and that's another reason I adore him. (You must pass Irony 101 to be my buddy.) This is his version of a close encounter with the New South.

> Dear Mil,
> I told you I was going to be visited by Cousin Randall, Great-uncle Randolph's great grandson, who just retired from the Army. He's only about forty—did you ever think we'd think of forty as "only"? Well, Cousin Randall came down to talk to Cousin Henry about the family business and stayed with us. After three days of seeing banks and lawyers, he asked me to take him down to Ninock, and then he was so fired up about family history, he wanted me to take him down to East Point, where the old house was before it fell into the river. I told him about the old graveyard on the place Henry sold to the Yankee doctor. We had a few beers, talked it over, and took ourselves through the fields to see it. It was afternoon, and there wasn't a soul in sight, and the gates were chained but not locked, so we pulled

Family Plot

up to the field beyond the little lake that borders the cemetery and got out and walked . . .

May I insert here that I am familiar with this field? I made the trck to the "old graveyard' in cold January, wearing my rubber boots and sticking in mud up to my shins with every step. I visited the holy, sacred, ancestral cemetery and made over the falling-down iron fence and the ancient gravestones and obelisks covered with black mold that a century and a half of weeping trees had dripped down. The little plot is isolated in what was once a cotton field, no sign of a path, nor of the homeplace that spawned it. Here are buried the wives of the patriarchs of Jimmy's family, along with some lesser others. (The patriarchs are elsewhere.) The graveyard was long ago abandoned. It evokes all too well the lost empire. The day I visited, we talked of what it would take to restore the fence, how relatively easy it would be to bleach the marble stones back to respectability, Jimmy vowing to cut the cedars and crape myrtles back so it wouldn't be so awfully dark and grim.

We spoke of eradicating the undergrowth, especially the rampant poison ivy, surely a plant brought down by the carpetbaggers to curse us forevermore! We stood on the ruined island of memory, surrounded by the dark brown earth of reality, and said all the things we wished we could do to preserve this piece of the past. When Henry sold it, Jimmy was devastated and blamed himself for not doing more . . .

Cousin Randall was ahead of me, and the field was planted with tall stuff, so my view of the cemetery was blocked. He saw it first. "Why," he said, "I thought you said it was pretty dilapidated. It looks O.K. to me."

The fence was pulled up and wired together and painted. The gravestones and obelisks gleamed, the trees had been pruned, and the poison ivy was gone. I couldn't get over it. We looked at all the graves, and I told cousin Randall who everyone was and where they

Family Plot

all fit into the family. We were still talking about it all, walking single file through the rows, when we came to the road where we'd parked. That's when we saw the Land Rover coming.

"Oh hell," I said to Cousin Randall. "The Yankees have got us! Don't worry, tho'. I know the sheriff. We aren't about to go to jail for trespassing in Red River Parish. Blood still counts for something here."

Then these three little boys, stairsteps, dressed completely in cowboy outfits, got out of the Rover. They had everything Western: boots, hats and all, and they ran toward us, then abruptly stopped about ten yards away.

"Lord, Randall, they're . . ." I began.

"Koreans", he finished.

Koreans??

He advanced toward the children and the Rover. The parents weren't far behind: slight, beautifully, but casually, dressed Asians. Their clothes and the Land Rover gave clear indication that these were people of means. The frowns they wore gave equally clear indication that they were none too pleased to find us here. I knew Henry had sold the farm to a pair of doctors from up north, but no one mentioned Koreans. (How did cousin Randall know they were Koreans, anyway?)

There Randall was, walking toward the two adults, now bowing deeply from the waist, now spouting a sing-song language that could be Korean, certainly sounded Asian; no way for me to know. (Who knew Cousin Randall spoke Korean?)

All of the sudden my role as the head of the family and official tour guide was wrested from me, and I was standing there, completely left out, not understanding a word being said. I ventured a "Hi", to the three kids, who said a shy "Hi", back.

Meanwhile, Cousin Randall and the two grown-ups were having a lengthy conversation, and he motioned to me to come. As I joined him, he hissed, "Bow."

"Bow?"

"Bow!" I bowed. He said something incomprehensible to the pair,

Family Plot

and I bowed again. (I was getting into this bowing stuff.) Mr. and Mrs.—actually, Doctor and Doctor—bowed back. Cousin Randall hissed, "Well, at least we aren't going to jail!" I smiled. I bowed again.

Introductions followed. Mrs. Doctor made me a touching little speech in rather good English to the effect that she and her husband were honored to have the responsibility of caring for our esteemed ancestors and would always provide care for the sacred burial place. I thanked her for honoring my humble family by making such a generous pledge, bowed some more, shook hands all round, solemnly, and we all left in our respective vehicles.

Well, it just goes to show that you never know. All these months I've been cussing Henry for selling the old home place, and it turns out it couldn't have been in better hands.. And how 'bout Cousin Randall? Who knew he'd been in Army Intelligence in the Far East and knew six Asian languages? He said that if you've been around Asian people a lot, it's easy to tell the nationalities apart. Easy for him to say. And how 'bout those three tiny cowboys? Surreal. Fully armed with little cap pistols, they never drew down on us trespassers. Talk about manners. My two little hellions would have been blazing away.

It's a wonderful world. I'm so relieved. Best of all, they were from South Korea, not even Yankees.

Sometimes things work out so well that you get a happy ending and a good tale. This is one for the book.

Death Notices

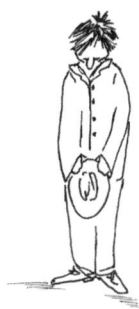

"Did you see the obituaries in the Advocate today?" Mama asked. We were having our first daily phone call at 10 A.M. I was at my office and had been for two hours. Mama was just rising. She couldn't sleep well at night since my daddy died. She "worked the dog" as my husband (who worked as a supervisor at a plant) used to say. She'd go to bed at 6 A.M.—after she'd read the paper.

"Yes, I saw that Meg Caldwell died."

"But, Baby, you obviously missed the wonderful irony. Vera Bingham died. The very same day. She'll be buried tomorrow. Here in Clay! At Pilgrim's Rest."

"My Lord, Mama, that is odd! How do you 'spose Cavalier's is gonna juggle the two services? Meg's is tomorrow, too."

"Meg at 10, Mrs. Bingham—altho' she's Mrs. Rosso now, or was—at 11:30. Of course, Meg will be buried at Roseneath. They have the family cemetery reserved even tho' the Caldwells lost it in '75. Should just about work, huh?"

"Do you 'spose Debbie will come, Mama?"

"Well, of course. Vera is her mother, after all."

"But she ran away all those years ago. And never came back."

"But I'll bet you she stayed in touch with Vera," Mama said. "Besides, those gypsies KNOW!"

"Oh, Mama."

"Well, Mary V., they do, and Vera's mama was a full-blooded

Death Notices

gypsy, gold hoop earrings, crystal ball and all."
"Yes, Mama, I remember . . ."

• • •

I remember the day Liz Caldwell and I snuck off from summer day-camp down at the Fairgrounds and dropped in on old Mrs. Cooper. We were nine. Liz's brother David had told us that Syrie Cooper read palms. We wanted to have our fortunes told, so when we were 'sposed to be gathering leaves to make a collage, we snuck across the creek to the Coopers' lot. Old Mrs. Cooper's son Felix lived in a trailer, but Syrie lived in a cabin, a shack really. We approached with delicious trepidation. The old oaks overhung the beaten dirt path and made it dark even at 11 in the morning. Mrs. Cooper heard our footsteps on her rickety porch. "Come in," she called.

Looking back from the distance of thirty-five years, I can just about say that Mrs. Cooper ("Madame Syrie. Call me Madame Syrie, cheel-drun," she had said.) was no more than an extraordinarily talented showman, probably a veteran of carnivals, skilled at presenting herself as a clairvoyant and woman of mystery, but to Liz and me, standing in her darkened parlor, chilly even in the July mid-day, she was an eerie apparition. We paid her a quarter each. (David had warned us that we must "cross her palm with silver.") She told our fortunes. Mine was lackluster, marriage to a nice man, two children—a boy and a girl, good fortune. I was pleased, but the inbred cynicism Mama had encouraged in me from birth led me to doubt the fortune was really mine. It was sort of generic, and I was let down. Then Madame Syrie took Liz's clammy paw.

"Oooh," said Madame with a sharply indrawn breath. One (if one had not been of a naturally suspicious vent) would have actually thought she had seen something there.

"What? What?" screeched Liz, pulling her hand away.

Death Notices

"Go away! Away from me, girl!" And we did, in a flash. We even picked up a few leaves in our flight back.

• • •

I remember when Liz and I were thirteen. David was seventeen, beginning his senior year, a football hero. I had been in love with him for years. We were up in the third-story ballroom at Roseneath, and he was teaching us to dance. Liz and I were going to attend our first sock-hop at the Legion Hall the Friday night after the first home game. David insisted he'd teach us how to dance so we wouldn't embarrass him. He declared everyone thought I was his little sister, too; Liz and I were inseparable; he'd have to teach us both. The record was Elvis's "Don't." David held me firmly. Of course, I could already dance. I'd taken lessons in grade school at Mrs. Little's, and Daddy had taught me to waltz and jitterbug to the Victrola. Dancing with David, tall and masterful, was not like either of those, however. At the end of the song he drew me close. Any number of new sensations presented themselves for my consideration. "Will you dance with me Friday night, David?" I breathed.

"Why sure, Little Sis. Somebody has to keep you and Liz from being wallflowers."

I was over the moon.

On the night, reality paled beside my fevered fantasies, for David had a date. Debbie Bingham was sixteen, petite, round of face and "fine" (She had impressive bosoms). She had long dark hair which she wore in a curled ponytail. She had big brown eyes and long lashes. She had deep dimples. She had a tiny waist, and she wore layers and layers of petticoats. Her dress was tacky, too much lace and too many ribbons, but she was adorable.

David did dance with both Liz and me, and so did a few of his friends, all senior boys and football players. The evening was OK, not a failure, but a long way from the evening of my dreams. David dropped us off at Roseneath (I was staying with Liz, of

Death Notices

course) before he took Debbie home. Liz dropped right off to sleep, but I lay awake until I heard David come in very late.

The Clay High School Panthers won the state football championship that year. Liz and I went to all the sock-hops, and we got to actually enjoying it after a while. David and Debbie had begun to go steady. She wore his junior football jacket and his senior ring on a chain around her neck. They danced beautifully together, she on tip-toe to hold her face up to his in the flickering, multicolored light from the ball in the center of the ceiling of the Legion Hall. It was at one of these dances that I first noticed something between the two of them that I was able to put a name to only later. It was the way they shared space. Even when they weren't touching, they caressed the air between them, they burned each other with their eyes. In years to come I would unfailingly identify passion between two people by these signs, but I first observed them then.

• • •

I remember a conversation I overheard between Mama and Mrs. Caldwell that Christmas at our house at their bridge club's Christmas party. Mrs. Caldwell was talking to Mama while Nanny and Bessie were cleaning up. The ladies were drinking Bourbon and smoking Marlboros, sitting in our den.

"What am I to do, Eugenia?" Mrs. Caldwell implored.

"Nothing you can do, Meg. Let it run its course," said Mama, ever the realist. "If it were your daughter, you could lock her up, send her to All Saints' or something, but David is a boy. Your hands are pretty much tied. Just hope he gets tired of her."

"But he adores her. He takes her everywhere. He took her to the Davises' Christmas party last Saturday night. He even wants to have her to our house for Christmas!"

"Well, be thankful he doesn't want to spend Christmas at the Binghams'!"

"Oh God, Eugenia! Gypsies!"

Death Notices

"Well, yes, Vera's mother . . ."
"And Bingham works at the sawmill."
"But the girl is adorable, Meg, you must admit."
"But trashy, Eugenia."
"But she adores David, and he, her."

Mrs. Caldwell flinched as if Mama had slapped her. "Well, I'll tell you this, Eugenia," she said, stubbing out her cigarette. "I'll not stand for a gypsy grandchild!"

• • •

I remember it was spring. Liz and I were standing out in front of the Joy Theatre. We'd just been to a double feature, but the titles evade me now. We were debating whether to walk home or call Daddy to come and get us, when Liz's Daddy drove up in his big Buick. He motioned for us to get in the car. His face was set in a grim mask.

"Liz, your mother sent me to get you."

"But, Daddy, I'm supposed to stay at Mary V.'s tonight."

"Your Mama wants you to come home, Baby, and Mary V. has to go to her house."

"Daddy, what . . .?" Liz began, but his look quelled her.

He pulled up at our gate and put the car in park. I remember that car so well. It was his first automatic transmission automobile, and he really loved it. He turned to us, cleared his throat, and said, "Girls, David and Debbie have just come in and told us that they have been married." We whooped. "And in the fall," he continued, "Debbie is going to have a little baby."

To this day the horrified look in Liz's eyes and the absolute nausea I felt come back to me as clear as day. Of course we could add two and two. We were almost fourteen! We had periods and everything. We had seen "A Summer Place," read *Harrison High*, and could count to nine, but in those long ago innocent times, getting pregnant and "having to get married" was shameful, not titillating. That David, our hero, our Galahad, our brother, had done

Death Notices

such a shameful deed was horrible to know. We cried for weeks.

David and Debbie moved into his room at Roseneath. Debbie was paler, and, by May she was pretty thick around the middle, but she finished her junior year of high school and David graduated.

During all that hot summer, as Debbie got bigger and bigger, Mrs. Caldwell fumed. Mama and Daddy commented on it regularly. Mama declared Meg was going absolutely crazy. After all, the baby was coming, a *fait accompli*. Why not make the best of it and help the kids along? And Daddy agreed, and said Mr. John was secretly delighted. He wanted a little girl for his first grandchild, Daddy said.

Over at Roseneath the house was full of fury and sex. Debbie, big as she was, was irresistible to David. Liz and I could hear them making love at night and early in the morning. Once when I was upstairs in Liz's room one afternoon looking for my bathing suit straps, the door to David's room cracked open (old houses settle), and I could see David and Debbie kneeling on his bed, David holding her breasts to his face. I nearly died.

"She'd better slack off," I heard Mama tell Ms. Caldwell. "She'll have that baby early if they keep it up." (No question in anyone's mind what "it" was.)

"I hope it does come early," replied Mrs. Caldwell vehemently, "and dies!"

At the beginning of August, old Mrs. Cooper died in her sleep. Felix Cooper insisted on a real gypsy funeral with relatives and friends coming from miles around and staying up day and night until the funeral, three days after the death. The Cavaliers were half crazy with what Marian Cavalier described to Mama as "the Romany hordes" camped out on the funeral home lawn, burning camp fires, playing guitars, the women keening. Mrs. Caldwell absolutely refused to go and pay her respects, but Mr. John, David, Liz and, of course, I went with Debbie every day. Vera Bingham sat by the coffin on a low stool, a dark shawl covering her head. Her husband, just a lost redneck Baptist adrift in

Death Notices

a sea of exotica, paced and smoked in the "lounge area." Finally, on the third night, the actual funeral came as an anti-climax, and Mrs. Cooper was buried in Pilgrim's Rest (the not-so-ritzy of the town's white cemeteries. All our folks were planted in Magnolia Hill.) by the light of the moon and stars. Marian and Chris Cavalier took a week off and went to the Gulf Coast while assistants cleaned up the funeral home, and Debbie woke up one morning reporting a dream in which her grandmother appeared to her and told her that the baby would be a girl and that she must be named "Syrie" "to keep her safe." As Debbie was usually such a down-to-earth, sunny girl, this turn of events was remarkable. Mrs. Caldwell raged that she would not have it, and David, Mr. John, and Liz went around oppressed.

It was awfully hot and stormy all that month as we waited for September and the baby. School started. Liz and I were freshmen. David began college, commuting fifty miles every morning. This development was a fresh source of irritation to Mrs. Caldwell who'd envisioned David at LSU pledging Kappa Alpha Order as his father and both grandfathers had done. David was showing the strain of his new role. He lost weight even as Debbie ballooned. The baby, far from being early, was overdue by a week. There was a storm in the Gulf, and, true to old wives' tales about low pressure bringing on labor, the baby was born the day the storm crossed the coast. Debbie was in labor for twenty-six hours. Mrs. Caldwell and David fought over whether David should go to school that day. He'd wanted to take her directly to the hospital. Between the thunder and the shouting, not to mention the pain, it's amazing Debbie didn't go crazy. By the time school was over that afternoon, and Liz and I went up to see her, she was in agony and terrified. Mrs. Caldwell had gone out after phoning Dr. Pierce, their obstetrician. He'd said there was no need to bring Debbie to the hospital until her labor pains were regular and ten minutes apart. Bessie and David were with her, and her Mama had been there and would return. Debbie thrashed when a contraction came (closer now and stronger) and lay sweat-

Death Notices

ing with fearful eyes after the pain subsided. Mr. John came home at 5, and Mrs. Bingham came back. She felt out of place in the big, ornately decorated bedroom, and she stood by the door despite Debbie's cries. One time she even cried out, "Mama, help me! Please help me!" but Mrs. Bingham only went to her side, held her hand and cried, big tears rolling down her sallow face. Mr. John paced out in the hall. Liz and I sat, horrified and speechless, on the window seat, afraid to stay or go. Somehow we were overlooked by the adults. By 6:30 Mr. John pronounced that enough was enough. Debbie had been in labor since early that morning. No doctor had seen her, and only Mrs. Caldwell had spoken with one, and she was nowhere to be found. Debbie was hysterical, and even Bessie, who'd delivered not a few babies herself and who'd given birth to five of her own, was looking concerned. After a whispered conversation with her, Mr. John went into action. He ordered Bessie and Mrs. Bingham to pack Debbie's things, freshen her up and prepare to take her to the Branton hospital. The bag was already packed, and there wasn't much freshening they could do in the fix Debbie was in, but we stepped out so they could change her gown and get a peignoir around her and get her up. It was only then, out in the hall, that Mr. John noticed Liz and me.

"Why, Elizabeth," he said, "You and Mary V. have no business . . . Oh, never mind! Elizabeth, go downstairs and call Dr. Pierce's house and tell him—don't ask him; tell him! that we're bringing Debbie in and for him to meet us there. Mary V. you go and get the Buick and bring it 'round to the front door. The front stairs are easier for us to negotiate."

We took off, glad not to be banished to the sidelines, gladder still to have something useful to do. I was gladder yet to be asked to bring Mr. John's beloved Buick around. Both Liz and I knew how to drive; my Daddy and David had both taught us, but to be asked to bring the Buick around in a moment of crisis! This demanded my very best behavior. I determined to be so careful. It's ironic what seems important when you're that age—and what you take for granted. We just knew Mr. John and Bessie would

Death Notices

make Debbie be OK.

They managed to get Debbie down the front staircase, Mr. John and David on each side of her, stopping every couple of steps. The thunder rolled outside.

"She shoulda been up walking before," Bessie said in a low voice, mostly to herself.

When Debbie got to the bottom step, her water broke. A huge gush of fluid poured from between her legs, wetting the gown and robe and the heart-pine floor. Bessie rushed toward the kitchen, presumably for a mop.

"NOW we're gettin' somewhere!" Mr. John exclaimed as Liz and I gaped, and Debbie blushed furiously. "Bessie, don't worry about that now! Get my plastic raincoat out of the hall closet and put it on the car seat. Hurry now!"

In no time they were gone, Debbie, her mother, David, and Mr. John. Bessie finally got to mop up the floor, but the fluid left spots. Liz and I vowed to remain childless forever.

Mrs. Caldwell came in about eight. She'd been at a bridge party, Mama told me later. She'd never even mentioned that Debbie was in labor.

The baby was born at 6 the next morning. They named her Syrie Margaret by way of compromise though Liz said Debbie said it went against the instructions in her dream. She had to be delivered by Caesarian section, and something was not right with her breathing. Then she developed pneumonia.

Debbie came home after five days, but Syrie Margaret stayed in the hospital. Debbie and David clung to each other. It seemed certain that the baby would die, but she lived. September passed into October. Then one morning Liz announced that the baby was coming home that day. The old nursery at the end of the hall was already prepared, just waiting. Mr. John and Bessie had fixed it according to Debbie's requests as she convalesced. It was all pink and white and furnished with Caldwell family antique baby furniture. Now the baby came to fill it.

Syrie was a beautiful baby with jet black hair and olive skin

Death Notices

and Debbie's dimples. Her eyes turned dark immediately.

"All she needs is a kerchief and gold earrings to be the spi't and image of old Mrs. Cooper," Margie Duncan said to Mama at the christening. "Meg must be mortified."

She was, and she was ever more furious because David and Mr. John adored the baby. Mrs. Bingham was around the house a lot, too, though she took pains to dodge Mrs. Caldwell.

David and Debbie were so happy. David made the Dean's List his first semester in college, and they planned to move into college housing at the end of the spring term.

Then the baby died. She just died. David was at school. Debbie had put Syrie down for a nap and was in their bedroom sewing. When she went to pick the baby up, Syrie was dead. Debbie went screaming for Bessie, and Liz, who'd stayed home from school with upset stomach, ran into the baby's room and then she began to scream, too. Mrs. Caldwell was out—nobody knew where she'd gone; she'd been around earlier—so Bessie called Mr. John, and he called Dr. Clay, but it was too late.

The saddest thing I ever saw was that tiny white coffin going into the earth at Pilgrim's Rest. Despite David's pleas, Debbie insisted they bury the baby there and not at Roseneath. She was hysterical about it, and she prevailed. The day was clear and lovely, cold—it was late February—but with the promise of spring to come. Only a few close friends were there, Mama and Daddy and me, of course; Dr. Clay and his wife (who'd been a Caldwell) and Mr. and Mrs. Abercrombie, Mr. John's sister and her husband; Bessie, Mr. and Mrs. Bingham, and Felix Cooper. Felix dug the grave by hand—such a sad little hole it was. Mr. Culpepper, the Presbyterian Minister, conducted the brief ceremony. He read the 23rd Psalm and said that part about "suffer the little children . . ." We all snuffled and cried. Then we went home.

Debbie refused to live at Roseneath after that. She went to her mother's until David could find an apartment at the college. To my knowledge she never set foot in the Caldwells' house again. When I said to Liz that this seemed really peculiar, Liz was

Death Notices

non-committal. She'd been pretty strange herself since Syrie died, and as good friends as we were, she wouldn't open up to me.

Actually, everything started to go bad for the Caldwells about then. Mr. John began to drink really bad. Mrs. Caldwell got colder and meaner. The family business (insurance) depended on Mr. John's reputation and clear thinking, and it declined. Liz took to going over to Claiborne and staying with Debbie and David every chance she got, and I wasn't invited. I gradually began to avoid Roseneath. It wasn't anything like the way it had been.

By the next fall David had quit school, and he and Debbie moved back to Clay. They both took jobs and were living in an old house down near the Binghams. Liz went off to All Saints' in Vicksburg. She said she wanted to. She rarely came home.

• • •

I remember the day David died. It was Hallowe'en, a Friday. We were at the gym decorating for a Hallowe'en Carnival during last period. The word swept through the hall. David had keeled over dead at the warehouse where he worked.

• • •

I remember the day Debbie disappeared. It was the day of the funeral. She just didn't appear. The whole town was there, but the young widow never came. After Mr. John and Daddy went looking for her and came back alone, the funeral took place. Daddy said all her personal things were gone from their little house, and so was their old car. Mr. John got the sheriff to put out an APB, but she was never found. She sold the car in McComb, Mississippi and just vanished.

• • •

I remember the day in 1970 when Liz died. She took pills—a

Death Notices

lot of pills. She was living in New Orleans then. I was married—to my own David—and living in Baton Rouge. Mama called me at work. I put my head down on my desk in full view of my four office mates and wept.

Mr. Bingham ran off with a barmaid, and Vera moved to Fillmore. She married a man named Rosso and had a baby, of all things. She was forty-five! She named the baby "David."

The Caldwells went from bad to worse. Mr. John died in DePaul's in New Orleans from cirrhosis, and Mrs. Caldwell sold Roseneath to the Fowlers. She moved into Baton Rouge and continued to enjoy society. Mama and I would see her at Mad Hatters' occasionally. She looked wonderful but was as mean as ever. When I married David Phillips, she sent me a crystal épergne and a nasty note saying she was sure I was destined to marry a David. Too bad the gypsies stole my original choice! I swear she did! Mama made me keep the épergne—and the note—much too good a souvenir to throw away out of pique, she said.

• • •

So here we were going to the wakes of both Margaret Caldwell and Vera Cooper Bingham Rosso. It is rare in a town as small as Clay for there to be two wakes at the same time, but the Cavaliers had room, having turned the old front porch into a second funeral parlor, their second best. Mrs. Rosso (naturally) lay in there, and Mrs. Caldwell lay in the first parlor. There were very few attendant at either place, but the class difference between the two was pronounced. The Rosso mourners wore shirt sleeves and slacks (men and women); the Caldwell crowd wore suits and dresses in somber shades. Mama and I wore navy blue, our usual funeral togs. We went to Meg's wake first. It was awfully sad. All her family just about had (as the obituaries say) "preceded her in death." There were only cousins there.

Vera Rosso's bier was surrounded by relatives. Felix Cooper was there, and Mr. Rosso, and—believe it—Mr. Bingham and his second wife. The son, David Rosso, a taller version of Felix Cooper, stood shyly in a corner. Lots of gypsy-looking (or—as Mama so correctly pointed out—Italian looking) folks inhabited the seating area, but Debbie was not to be seen. I was very disappointed.

I had a big deadline the next day and so did not attend Meg Caldwell's funeral, but Mama did, and, in her second daily call to me (at 2 P.M.) she filled me in on who was there and who wore what and what they said.

". . .And you know, Baby, since your Daddy died I don't go to graveyards, but since I was with Marcie, and she wanted to go, I just said 'What the hell?' and went, and do you know? I could swear I saw David Caldwell—Yes, Mary V., I know he's been dead lo' these nearly thirty years, but I swear . . ."

Someone who looked a very great deal like David had been in the family plot near David's grave as the hearse and mourners drew up. Then he had "vanished." Curious!

That evening, as I was driving home (having gone all over town running errands after work) I passed the cemetery—Pilgrim's Rest, I mean—and there, coming down the gravel path, were David and Debbie. The light was failing, but I knew they were flesh and blood, not ghosts, and, besides, there was a young blonde woman with them, and she did not look a thing in the world like anyone I knew. I stomped on the brakes and backed down the Branton Road until I drew up even with them as they reached their car.

When the dust cleared, I was sitting in the bar of the "Roseneath Inn" having a gin and tonic with Debbie Bingham Caldwell. Her son, David, and his delightful wife, Sara, had diplomatically excused themselves and left Debbie and me to discuss the past thirty years.

"She killed them, you know. Meg Caldwell killed them all, David, Liz, Mr. John . . ., but first of all, she killed my Syrie." There was no preface, no small talk, and surely no way to stem the tide of Debbie's narrative, not that I wanted to. Debbie was earnest, not hysterical. She spoke in a low, calm voice, but the only other people in the room were the bartender and the waitress, and they were engrossed in each other.

"Funny, isn't it?" Debbie continued, "This was the sun porch. Mr. John kept all his plants out here, you remember?" I nodded. "I used to sit out here when I was so big pregnant. There was a glider. I could put my feet up and swing. Most of all, I could be alone. Meg would never come out here. She said the plants aggravated her allergies . . . Anyway, as I was telling you, she killed Syrie. And Liz and Mr. John both knew it. Liz almost caught her doing it.

"You remember, Liz stayed home that day. She had stomach flu. We'd all had it, but Syrie hadn't gotten it. I was scared to death she would—she'd had such a rough start—but she was fine. I put her down for a nap at 1 and went into our room to sew. Meg was in her room. She was just getting over the flu and felt pretty weak, but she told me not to worry. If the baby cried, she'd go in and check her; her room was closer to the nursery than ours.

"I heard Syrie cry out about 2, and I heard Meg go down the hall, and Syrie stopped crying after a few minutes. Then I heard somebody come out of the big bathroom, and a door open and close, and then someone went down the back stairs. I guess I sewed another few minutes, and then I put all the sewing things away, and then I folded the clothes I'd mended and stacked them to take down to Bessie's pantry to be ironed. Then I went down the hall to get my baby.

"At first I just thought she was asleep. She was still warm. I picked her up, and she was so limp. I knew then, and I screamed and screamed. Then Liz came, and as soon as she saw Syrie, she just stood stock still—frozen—and she said 'She's dead, isn't she?' I'll never forget that. I didn't understand at the time how she knew, but I kept seeing her face and kept hearing her say 'She's dead, isn't she?' How could she have known?

"She came to me that night. I was out on the back porch in the cold, rocking. David and Mr. John had gone to the funeral home. Meg was—I don't know where she was. Liz didn't tell me then. She just sat with me, and we talked about Syrie, how pretty she was, and how much fun to play with, and what all we'd hoped for her, and Liz said, 'Deb, put her with your Grandma at Pilgrim's Rest. Don't let Mama keep her here,' and the way she said it, I knew. I just knew."

"When?" I said. It was all I could say. "I guess Liz saw Meg . . ."

"Bent over the baby's crib with the pillow. You remember we fought about that baby pillow? It had been David's and Liz's, but Dr. Clay said babies shouldn't use pillows . . . Anyway, Meg went down the back stairs and out of the house and away, and Liz didn't absorb what she'd seen until it dawned on her that Syrie was dead."

"So you buried Syrie beside Mrs. Cooper and moved out of Roseneath."

"And never set foot in this place again until yesterday. The people that bought it have done a nice job converting it. I thought I could bear to stay here now, had to stay someplace for Mama's funeral, and besides, I wanted David to see it. It's his father's family's home."

"About David?" I asked. "This David. Your son, I mean."

"I was pregnant with him when David died. I had just found out. I'm so glad David knew before he died. We'd wanted another baby so much."

"But how did you get away?"

"Mr. John. He knew everything. Liz'd finally told us both. He gave us money, that old car. He was so good. He was a gentle, gentle man. When David died, I told him I couldn't stay in Clay any longer. He understood. He fixed it up for me to go to Memphis to some friends, and he sent me money as long as he lived. He knew I'd had a son, but he never saw him. Neither did Liz. While she was in Vicksburg, I used to call her, but she would never come and visit us.

"Mr. John paid for me to take a business course, and that's

how I've supported myself. I'm the manager of a plumbing supply company in Memphis, and David's an accountant. He and Sara have their own firm, but no children. Either they can't, or they don't want to. It's their business. They don't say, and I don't ask. I try to be a better mother-in-law than the one I had."

"But, David—your husband David—you said Meg killed him, too."

"I guess that was a little out of line. She didn't kill him outright. He died of an abdominal aneurysm that ruptured. We never knew he had it. He just died. The autopsy showed it, and Mr. John said Meg's father and aunt both died of that, too, so it was in her family. I guess that was pretty bitter to her. David was the only person she ever really loved."

"Meg Caldwell died of a ruptured abdominal aneurysm," I said.

"I know. Sort of poetic, huh?"

• • •

I remember a conversation Liz and I had just before she went off to All Saints'. We were talking about having children. I wanted six. She had always wanted a big family, too, but that day she declared she'd never marry, never have children. It shocked me at the time, and I tried to get at what had changed her mind. Now I think, what if she had told me? What would I have done if she had up and said, "I don't want to have any children because my mother is a murderess. She killed my niece." I don't know. I was all of sixteen. I doubt I could've said anything to help, anything that would've changed the path she took and the way she died, but oh Lord, I wish I'd've had that option. You see, even after all these years, I can read Liz—we were so close for so long. Liz knew. She knew her mother was killing Syrie. She saw it. She didn't "almost" catch Meg. Meg was in the act as Liz passed out of the big bathroom beside the nursery and crossed the hall to her room. Liz knew, and for whatever reason: denial, jealousy of her

Death Notices

beloved brother's love for Deb and Syrie, wanting her Mama's approval—whatever, she "passed by on the other side" and loathed herself thereafter.

All of this I told to Mama during our fourth (and last) phone call of that strange, eventful day.

"Don't grieve, Mary V.," Mama said. "It's in the Lord's hands now, and He will sort it out."

When my down-to-earth Mama starts with the Southern religious wisdom, I know she's been thrown a curve.

"What's buggin' you, Ma?" I asked baldly.

"Your Daddy knew, Mary V. Dollars to doughnuts Jack knew. And he never told me!"

Daddy didn't keep many secrets from Mama. She was too sharp, and he was too easily probed.

"Don't grieve, Mama," I said. "In the sweet bye and bye—"

"I'll get him!" said Mama firmly, and hung up.

Paschal Feast

"I hope you have a good idea what you're letting yourself in for," David yelled. "I just hope you can imagine how awful it's going to be. You should know my mother by now. You should have at least an inkling . . ."

"I promised Father Sloane, David. I gave him my solemn word, we all did, all the choir, long before any of this came up. We promised we'd be here to sing for Holy Week and Easter."

"Damn Father Sloane and your half-assed choir. I want you to miss all this misery. I want you to go to Grand Isle with me."

"And I would, if only you would wait to go until 10 o'clock on Easter morning."

"Hell, no! I'm not waiting around here and take the chance of being caught and having to stay here for Mama's crazy barbecue just so you can sing. If you want to, Vicky, you can save yourself. I'm saving me!"

In the end, David departed on Maundy Thursday at noon with a grim but tearless Victoria kissing him goodbye and promising him she'd break for Grand Isle directly after church on Easter Sunday. They both knew she would never do it, but they politely maintained the fiction until David's old truck was out of sight.

Sunday was fair and mild, a picture-book Easter. Victoria, precluded by choir duty from sporting new Easter finery, nevertheless felt festive as she waited outside the picturesque Victorian

Paschal Feast

church for Easter Day services to begin with the procession of choir and acolytes, crucifer, and clergy. Father Sloane, nervous, dyspeptic, and rigid (one of the other choir members described him aptly as a "white-knuckled recent post-seminarian") darted about getting every procession participant into place. The magnificent organ boomed out the processional, and they were "off", finally, but just as the choir was leaving the vestibule in procession, David's brother, Chris, slipped into a rear pew, leaving behind him the overpowering combined scents of Lagerfeld and Scotch. A tremor passed over Victoria. Her Mama would have said that a rabbit had run over her grave.

Mrs. Collins' Easter barbecue was an annual event, attended by family and carefully chosen invited guests possessing only the best social credentials. It was as fixed as sunrise service (which the Collinses, being High Episcopalians, never attended) and the town Easter Egg Hunt. Invitations were greatly sought after. Even mourning for a family member did not interfere, as Victoria had discovered rather sadly after hers and David's only child, their ten year old son, Hugh, died in late February in a year when Easter came early. Her absence from the party had been severely censured, Mrs. Collins having been heard to say that Collinses were able to transcend loss and do their duty. Victoria was crushed, but she got the message. David had never attended since. This year, a living sorrow, David's sister Clare, comatose and on a respirator since an automobile accident months earlier, was not even excused from attendance. Indeed, horribly, she was to be the centerpiece of the event.

Margaret Fowler Collins was stone crazy. Of this Victoria had been convinced for some time, but her producing the exhibition of Clare, transported from the skilled care facility where she existed only supported by vast mechanical assistance, was installed, respirator, electric bed, undulating, variable-pressure air mattress and all, under a yellow and white marquee in the garden of Fairhaven, for all the carefully-vetted guests to see. This had to be an unbeatable new low. Oddly, people seemed to take it in

Paschal Feast

stride, stepping over the cables connecting the respirator, bed, mattress pump, etc. to a portable generator, in order to brush Clare's lifeless face with their hands or lips. They made inane, complimentary remarks to Margaret about the bower of flowers ("Lilies, DAH-ling, how lovely—and so appropriate.") that surrounded Clare. Was Victoria the only one that thought the set up resembled nothing so much as a bier? God knew Clare had given Margaret not a moment's peace or satisfaction when she was up and going. Maybe this was the only way she was compelled to be still and presentable. A terrible thought: was this some form of revenge?

Chris materialized at Victoria's ear and hissed, "Be glad you were spared the grand entrance with ambulance and hand-cranked respirator." How, she wondered, could his nauseating scents be even stronger here in the out of doors than in church, but they were.

She turned on him angrily. "How can your Mama do this?" she demanded.

"Couldn't possibly say, DAH-ling," he replied. "Maybe revenge. Maybe this is the only way she knows to have fun. She is a bit bizarre at her best." He turned away.

Victoria was disgusted and repelled. Tables groaning under fabulous food; the best champagne or liquors to drink; the Æolian Harp String Ensemble playing away on the lawn, almost drowning out the compressed hiss of the respirator. In a moment, Victoria felt dizzy and sick. The whole Collins ethos was too much for her. She came from nice people. She'd made David a good wife. She had been an exemplary mother to Hugh for the brief time she'd had him in her care, but none of this was enough. She could never fit into this three ring circus. Still she was bound. David blew them off: Margaret and her cloying demands, the embarrassment of Chris, the tragedy of Clare. Since Hugh died, nothing seemed to touch David, and she certainly couldn't. Neither could she escape as he managed to do. "What a wuss!" she thought. She'd never measure up, but she kept trying. She didn't want to be like Margaret. What did she want? To fit in? How could she ever do that? What made Margaret tick? Had she always been so cold? Too many questions and a distinct shortage of any usable answers made Victoria's head ache.

Fortunately, there was no shortage of her favorite white wine, and the perfectly trained wine steward never batted an eye when she asked him to open a large bottle and give it to her with only one glass. It was advantageous to be Miss Victoria, Mr. David's lady, with the excellent servants Margaret engaged. Victoria nodded and bowed as she made her way towards the fields and woods behind the house. There were dear memories in these woods, memories of Hugh and David and better days. She had even had a laugh or two with Clare, swimming in the old pond on lazy days when Clare was between marriages and living at home.

The pond was well hidden from the house and formal garden. It was reached by rough paths, overgrown now by blackberry briars, but when she reached it, it still looked inviting, shady on one side, and the water was cool, not cold. She set the wine down in the water and propped it. She took off her shoes and dangled her feet in the water. She lay on the old pier and looked up at the trees and sky. She drank more wine.

A very loud shot awoke her, although she was sure she hadn't really been sleeping. It was Chris, shooting at box turtles on a log, a weasley thing to do, but the turtles were in little or no danger. Chris was so drunk he couldn't have hit the ground with his hat, but he was waving the pistol around dangerously. Chris's persona contained a cesspool of anger, she'd always known, but she'd never seen him armed before. Usually, he mocked David and the "manly men" (as he called them) who liked guns and hunting.

"Chris," she cried out, "what's with the gun?"

"Like it, sister-in-law?" he shouted back at her, and he fired another round vaguely at the log. It hit a big stone on the bank and ricocheted. "Oops!" he said, sheepishly. "Guess I need to keep my powder dry. I might really want to waste somebody, and then I might be out of firepower."

"Chris, you idiot, put that damn gun down."

"Whassa matter, V? 'Fraid I'll shoot you? Wuddn't ever shoot you, sister-in-law. You not a Collins. Only Collins blood bad. Oh, yeah, and Fowler. Fowlers are the worst. Mama said the worst thing about Clare was, she was named for old Grandma Fowler, and she was just as full of hell as Grandma Fowler. Well, Sister's not much full of hell anymore, is she? She's full of tubes, and Mama's full of meanness. Still, I guess ol' Clare brought it on herself. She should've died and deprived Mama of the chance to do this lugubrious production. It's really all Clare's fault, or my fault, or David's fault . . . Hell, David's figured it out. He's escaped, V. Mama can't hurt him or embarrass him any more. He doesn't even mind having a drunk queer for a brother. He's outta here. He's gone somewhere else. Wish I could go somewhere else, don't you?"

Instead, he made a beeline for the dock and her wine. He drank most of it while she shot the gun ("a Glock, not just a gun!") When the casings ejected, you had to be really careful. They were hot, and if they landed down your décolletage, they burned right smart. Chris and Victoria had a few laughs about that, the first laughs Victoria'd been able to get out of the day so far.

"Guess I'll go back and tend to Clare and Mama, " Chris finally said. "Walk you back?"

"No. I think I'll stay down here awhile." Victoria was mellow from the wine and remembering other afternoons by the pond. The episode with Chris had, oddly, brought her some respite. He was entirely strange, and thoroughly messed up, but he was kind and funny and very bright. She lay back on the pier and listened. The sun was going down. The frogs were tuning up.

What was that? More shots? Jolted out of her stupor, she jumped up. It was getting dark, and Victoria could barely see the path, but she hurried. She wasn't sure what had alarmed her, but she tore her dress any number of times fleeing through the briars. As she came up the hill into the garden, she ran faster because people were screaming. She tore around the corner of the marquee.

Paschal Feast

Spot lights (also generator-run) illuminated the scene like a shopping mall parking lot. As she entered the tent, the crowd hushed, and Victoria could hear the silence. Total silence. No one seemed to breathe. Her first visual impression was of lilies painted red. This resolved itself into Mrs. Collins lying in a stand of lilies, bleeding all over them from a fist-sized wound squarely in her center. Chris lay over Clare, motionless, the left side of his head missing. The Glock lay as it had fallen on the ground, just below the bed. Clare was no longer breathing; that is, the respirator no longer hissed and pumped air into her lungs. It was turned "OFF."

Victoria was rather proud of herself. She didn't scream. She didn't faint. She didn't call for David in Grand Isle, at least not then. She called for Father Sloane, the Sheriff, and the servants. She asked for a glass of cool water and some aspirin. She accepted condolences. She presided over the disaster, and she didn't flinch. Finally worthy to be a Collins! Margaret herself could not have handled it more cooly.

Aunt Lu
The Funeral Aunt

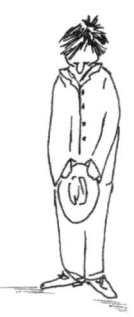

Aunt Lu (short for LewEllyn) was my father's great-aunt, and we called her "the Funeral Aunt." She was a posthumous child of my great-great grandfather, Lewellyn Morgan by his third wife. Great-great Grandpa Lewellyn was a prodigious sire, begetting twenty children by three wives, killing the first two from "female complications" in the process and surviving all of his progeny but three when he died at age seventy in 1888. Aunt Lu was born four months later, in February, 1889. She was considered from the first a child of sorrow. Her young mother died when Lu was just five, and Lu was sent to live with her half-brother, David, and his wife because they had a son almost exactly her age. This son, Hugh David, was to become my grandfather. He and Lu were raised as brother and sister, and he remained close to her his entire life, so much so that Lu always considered Grandpa's home her home and retired to it in her four periods of widowhood. She married for the first time in 1912, and was widowed in 1917. Her first husband had the unsought distinction of being among the first American casualties of World War I. He did, however, leave her comfortably off. Her second husband was slightly younger than she. He was the scion of an Eastern banking family who jumped out of a window in the Crash of 1929. His suicide was precipitate, however. He was not, as he had

The Funeral Aunt

thought, ruined. Lu inherited oil money from him. Husband number three was an officer in the Navy. He died at Pearl Harbor. Lu was devastated. They'd married after a whirlwind courtship. He had quite swept her off her feet. Her last husband was the only one I knew, Uncle Hardy. She married him the year my brother was born, 1946, and everyone in the family loved him. When I came along, in 1948, he became my godfather. He owned car dealerships all over the place, and he always drove a brand new car. He died when I was eight. That was when Aunt Lu came to live with Grandma and Grandpa for good.

My family, the Morgans, were Welsh. The Morgans were short, dark, musical, and given to temper and flights of fancy. Aunt Lu was, in all these traits, pure Morgan. In addition, she was fey. In the family it was recognized that Lu was a sensitive, sometimes clairvoyant. She never claimed this trait herself. She demonstrated it on any number of occasions. In Grandpa's house, the old Morgan home, she had her own set of rooms. Wealthy from her four husbands, she maintained the house with her funds. Grandpa paid for the utilities and food, Aunt Lu paid to have the old frame house painted every year, updated the plumbing and electrical wiring, fixed the roof when it was called for. She also had her own servants, Rachel and Jack Dempsey Thomas, who lived in a house in the back yard. Grandma had Ollie, her cook, and there was also Moses, who worked in the yard and drove Grandpa after he had his first stroke in 1955, but they didn't live on the place. All in all, Grandpa, Grandma and Aunt Lu all got along famously, although, after Grandpa died in 1958, I think Grandma went through a bad time of wishing she had the whole place to herself, but mostly everybody rocked along happily.

We children adored Aunt Lu. Despite the fact that she always wore unrelieved black and rarely went out, she was the most inventive and creative person when it came to playing with children. She taught us origami, making us listen as she read from books first, "to give you the basics." One Christmas she had an origami tree, totally decorated with our figures. She was musical

The Funeral Aunt

and had a baby grand piano, a gift from "Number 2," as she referred to her second husband. ("No need for you children to remember the first three names," she would say lightly. "You never knew them, only dear Hardy.") She would line us all up—there were five of us: me, my brother, Mac; Rachel and Jack's Cicely, our cousins Beth and Wooly (Albert)—and have us sing rounds or carols, whatever she fancied that day. Cicely never could sing, and Beth had a voice like an angel, and the rest of us were just so-so, but it was always fun when she got us together. She tried to teach us a little Welsh because all the Morgans could manage a tiny bit of it until Mac and me. It is a lovely language, but difficult for southern English speakers to get their tongues around. Actually, Cicely did the best, a predictor of her facility for languages that enabled her to get her Ph. D. in linguistics. Most days in vacation time would find us knocking on her sitting room door on the side porch. We'd spend an hour or so with her, but, as she rarely ventured out, except to church and such, we'd soon abandon her company for the joys of all outdoors. In bad weather, however, we hovered around her all day. She had a working fireplace in her sitting room, and we'd toast bread or roast weenies or marshmallows, and Rachel made the best hot chocolate in the world. We'd sit around on the Oriental rugs

The Funeral Aunt

("Priceless," my Mama would tell Daddy, "and she lets those kids and dogs and cats loll around on them and eat over them as if they were croker sacks!") and she'd read to us from her vast library. Ultimately, however, every visit would climax with a perusal of her scrapbooks and family pictures.

Aunt Lu always wore black, but she compensated for that in her design of scrapbooks. These volumes, which she began to assemble as a small girl, were brilliant and full of life and color. The materials she used were eclectic; anything from actual fabrics and original sketches to newspaper and magazine articles and illustrations to her own delicately handwritten poems and prose were put together with such an eye for design and with such creativeness that even we children recognized them for what they were: true art. As counterpoint to the scrapbooks, which had lively themes, there were the rather terrifying family photographs, for Aunt Lu had inherited the Morgan collection, and these included numerous daguerrotypes and sepia prints of dead people. Not people who were currently dead. People who were dead when the pictures were taken. There were any number of dead infants and toddlers. Remember, Aunt Lu was the last of twenty, only three of whom were still alive when she was born. The family explained that so many of the pictures of dead infants were taken for their despondent mothers, who, after the ordeals of childbirth, were often so debilitated that they never were able to hold their newborns in their arms before the children died. We couldn't even begin to understand such discussion. We were just children who thrived on horrors and lugubrious images, and we begged to see the collection—and hear all the stories ("This is my baby brother who was born dead. This is my half-sister, Margaret Owen. She died of typhoid when she was six. This is my poor mother. She had an apoplexy and died when she was only twenty-five and I was only five . . .") which never varied—every time we visited for any extended period of stay. If I close my eyes and tilt my head just a certain way, I can see, hear, and smell the exact way we'd be there in her sitting room, the fire blazing away, her

The Funeral Aunt

bell-like voice full of beauty and sadness, the smell of the wood smoke and the rugs and the dogs and cats. We were enthralled.

How she came to conduct our childhood burial services was serendipitous. We knew that she was famous in our town and family for attending funerals. These services were, indeed, the only occasions upon which she invariably bestowed her presence. She went to church (all the Morgans were devout Methodists until my Father married my Mama, and she imposed Episcopalianism on Mac and me) on an irregular schedule, mostly dictated by the weather, but she never missed a funeral among the white community's deceased, and she, accompanied by Rachel and driven by Jack Dempsey, went to many "colored" obsequies. At these, she was ever greeted at the vestibule and deferentially escorted by the pastor or other elder up to a place of honor near the front. All through her lifetime this honor was hers. Even when the Civil Rights era arrived in our little town, and Black Power flags and enormous Afro's were a feature of funerals, Aunt Lu got the same treatment. Rachel said she was revered for her calm acceptance of death and her faithful honoring of the dead. Whatever it was, when the first Black mayor of our town died, I, who had been one of his staunchest and earliest supporters, got to the funeral late and had to stand along the church wall (with lots of others, Black and White) while Aunt Lu, arriving even later, was escorted to her accustomed pew. This was the last but one funeral that she attended, but I need to back up.

The pet funerals: it started this way. Mac had a turtle. He'd captured it down by the little creek that ran in back of our house, and he fell in love with the thing. He must have been six or seven because I was five. The turtle actually lived for a reasonable spell and might have lived longer, but Daddy rolled over it with his truck, and that was the end of "Tom." Mac—and I, as I was his devoted worshipper at that stage of our childhood—cried buckets. We wrapped the remains of Tom in an old croker sack and set out to inter him in the back yard. We summoned Beth and Cicely and Wooly and were preparing for the funeral when Wooly sug-

The Funeral Aunt

gested we ought to go and see if Aunt Lu (who just loved funerals) would come and preside so that we could put Tom away in proper style.

"She won't come," Mac said, tearfully. "She never comes over here."

"Miss Lu never misses a funeral," Cicely rejoined, so we went.

Aunt Lu readily agreed to our invitation, making only one request. She preferred that we inter Tom in her back garden where she had already established her own cemetery for beloved pets who had passed away. Mac as the nearest bereaved got to decide, and he was delighted. We were all vaguely aware of the little plot in the rear of Grandma's house that Jack Dempsey tended into a cutting and herb garden under Aunt Lu's directions, but we must never have realized that behind it, next to the fence, were many little mounds with each grave marked by a piece of brick or stone. Aunt Lu quickly gave us a tour, and, not surprisingly, she was able to identify each pet and recall endearing traits as she told us about them. There were cats, dogs, rabbits, and even another turtle, pets of her early childhood when she lived in the family home before she married and every one that had died since she returned to the house in her widowhood. It was no small collection.

"Let's put Tom here," suggested Aunt Lu, indicating the spot directly in front of the mound she'd told us contained her own former pet turtle, Æsop. "I think it will be a suitable place." So we did. Mac stood back, as befitted the chief mourner, and let Wooly dig the hole as he clutched Tom in his croker sack shroud close.

"Now, Mac," said Aunt Lu when the hole was pronounced appropriate, "put Tom to rest." At first I thought Mac would refuse to part with the bundle, he looked so stricken. (Years later, when we buried Daddy, he would tell me that the moment he had to part with what had been Tom was the moment that he truly appreciated the enormity of death—and the moment he began to want to become a priest.) Then he rallied and gently placed Tom

The Funeral Aunt

and all into the ground. I believe all we children breathed a silent sigh of relief.

"Now we must say a few reverent words over our departed friend, Tom," continued Aunt Lu in her best funeral-director voice. "Who wants to go first?" Well, none of us had ever even been to a funeral before, so we stood dumb. "Very well," she continued. I shall do it." Then she cleared her throat gently and folded her hands and bowed her head. We followed suit.

"Dear Lord," she intoned, "please accept our pet, Tom, into Your kingdom. We loved him, and we trust You love him also, as he was one of Your creatures. We trust You to watch over him and keep him close to You. Amen." It was perfect.

"Now," she said, "we must sing."

We all looked around at each other until Beth, our gifted vocalist, began in a fine though wavering voice "All Things Bright and Beautiful." We joined in, as we all knew the words from the various Children's Day and Bible School programs. At the end, Aunt Lu reached for the shovel and filled in the grave very matter-of-factly, dusting off her hands and gathering us up to go. As we trooped back to her house for lemonade and graham crackers, she complimented us all in turn. "The hymn was perfect, Beth," she stated, "and all of you sang so well. Wooly, you were a won-

The Funeral Aunt

derful grave digger. I know Mac appreciated it, and Cicely, the zinnias from the garden were just the right thing for a tribute, and Meg (this as she patted me on my arm) you were so loyal and steadfast as your brother's chief supporter. Yes, dears, an altogether fine funeral for our friend. And now we must have something to eat and drink in honor of Tom, and then Life Must Go On."

This was, then, to become our pattern. It was only the first of many pet interments over which Aunt Lu presided during our collective childhood. Mac and I lived on a busy main street, and our cats and dogs were always coming to grief. Beth had chickens for 4-H, and the ones that didn't get fried were always dying. We finally had a special bird plot which came to hold my albino parakeet, Snow White, and Cicely's two canaries, as well as Easter ducklings that didn't live past Ascension Sunday, and the other fowl casualties. Eventually, the pet plots moved around the entire fence, and we took to begging the local funeral homes for those tin temporary grave markers so we could keep all the dearly departed straight—and know where next to dig. As we grew from childhood into adolescence, the number of pets declined, but the intensity of grief when one would die increased. The very worst was Wooly's dog, Beau. Wooly got Beau when he was eight, and Beau lived to be twelve. He died just as Wooly was preparing to go overseas to Vietnam, the only one of our intimate circle to be drafted. It was a terrible blow, only amplified by our foreboding about Wooly's future. He was all fired up and supported the war (which none of the rest of us did at all, including Aunt Lu, who'd been widowed by two conflicts) and didn't seem to mind going, but losing Beau right at that juncture brought all his repressed fears and grief to the surface. We appealed to Aunt Lu to comfort him and arranged the interment for the next day. As luck would have it, Cicely was home from graduate school at Georgetown for a summer break, and our little band gathered out in the back yard to bury Beau. Wooly's mother and dad, shaken by the concatenation of events, attended, as did my parents and Rachel and Jack

The Funeral Aunt

Dempsey. By this time, 1968, Grandpa was gone and Grandma was on her last legs. I remember she was looking out of her bedroom window while we performed the sad ceremony. It went according to our patented Order of Service, essentially unchanged since we first used it to bury Tom all those years before. This time Mac said the committal prayer, entrusting Beau, our faithful friend, to God's loving care. Beth led the singing, as usual, and Cicely had made a wreath of eucalyptus. I just cried. It was the end of childhood to me. Beau'd been part and parcel of our lives for all those years, and now he was gone, and Wooly was going. I wept uncontrollably until Aunt Lu herself, frail with age yet strong in her sense of the right thing to do, took control of me and led me back to her sitting room even before the grave was closed. She wet a towel and wiped my face and said, "You saw it, too, Meg. You have the sight a little bit." I knew exactly what she meant: the sight. The dark Welsh ability to grasp a glimpse of the future, clairvoyance. A gift, but what a heavy burden. I merely nodded, and we spoke no more of it and recovered ourselves in time to greet the other mourners with food and drink, and so the terrible funeral was carried off successfully.

Wooly lasted just thirty-five days "in country." He was killed and shipped home before we even got the marker from O'Hara's for Beau's grave. Remarkable fortitude was all that allowed Aunt Lu to endure the seemingly interminable military graveside services, but she held the rest of our tiny circle together until everyone else had left, and then, as we stood holding hands, she led us in the one of our ceremonies. This time the committal prayer was amended to express our faith that Wooly (never "Albert" to us; he hated the name) was with God the Father in the presence of God the Son and God the Holy Ghost and that we would all be together again in Heaven. Beth led us in "Amazing Grace," and we ended by each saying a simple farewell.

After Wooly died, it took Aunt Lu a good bit of time before she was her old self, attending funerals left and right, but she did recover. "Death is all part of it, Meg," she told me often that fall

The Funeral Aunt

and winter. My whole life has been surrounded by death, but Life Goes On to the end."

Having occasional flashes of clairvoyance receded into the background as I attended college, went to work, got married. However, the night before my wedding to Steve, the nicest man I never should have married in the first place, I was treated to one of the insights I'd rather not have received from the great cosmos. In it I saw myself packing boxes and crying, and, indeed, it happened just that way only three years later when it became apparent that Steve and I were not an even acceptable match for each other. We had, thankfully, no children, so I returned home and went to work for the only person who'd give me a job, Cicely's cousin Crowder Williams who was running an anti-poverty program. This was 1974. In 1978, Crowder ran for mayor of our town and was elected. I took over the program and ran it until it merged with a regional one in 1994. Crowder held the Mayor's post until he died, far too young, in 1982. His was the funeral where I stood along the wall, and Aunt Lu sat in her accustomed honored position.

Rachel died at the end of October, 1983. She was only seventy and had always enjoyed robust health, but she got cancer and lived only a few weeks after it was diagnosed. Aunt Lu was then almost ninety-five, but she nursed Rachel as best she could, assisted (because thanks to Beth's becoming an investment counselor and banker even though she was felt to be destined for the musical field, Aunt Lu's considerable inheritances had grown to the mass of great fortune) by a number of well-paid and very capable caregivers. Rachel had long since moved into the main house which had become Aunt Lu's after Grandma died, and she died in her own room. "It was, I suppose, an easy death," said Aunt Lu when she called me to tell me, "easy, I think for Rachel, but the hardest of all for me." As we had done for Wooly and for Jack Dempsey and for Grandma and for Daddy, we made our circle and said our ceremony. I assisted Aunt Lu back into her car, driven this time by me. The funeral baked meats were served at Aunt

The Funeral Aunt

Lu's, of course, as the house was the only home Rachel had known for over thirty years, and Cicely lived in Nashville. The crowd was not that large, and the eating and visiting was not prolonged. I remained behind to get Aunt Lu settled. I stayed over that night and have lived in the house ever since. It just seemed to evolve. I abandoned my own little house gladly. I never could adjust to living in a "new" structure, and I would not live with Mama. Mac was married and about to move up in the Episcopal hierarchy, and it was doubtful he'd ever want to come home, but Mama was holding out hope that one of us would want her home after she was gone. Not I.

In the next weeks, Aunt Lu put her affairs in order. She went about it all in a most dispassionate and business-like manner. We never spoke of her impending death, but we prepared. She left her house, the "old Morgan home," to me. She divided her estate, leaving all of us something and plenty to the Methodist Church and our local animal welfare people. She took out all the scrapbooks—which she continued to make right up until Rachel got sick—and all the family stuff and labeled it all and wrote notes and explanations and entrusted it all to me. I was to be the keeper of the family treasures—and the family pet plots. We took a last walk around the fence together on an unusually cold morning in late November. I wanted to wait for a better day, or at least for later in the day, but she was adamant. We identified most of our pets, but for once, Aunt Lu's memory failed her. As we regressed to the original plots, she began to falter and couldn't say if this was Chip or Cuddles or even what species was there. She looked up at me with her big brown eyes glistening with tears. We went back into the house, and she never left it again.

The last night of her life she was very chipper, talkative, very sharp. She told me she'd never regretted having no children, that she truly preferred animals—"except for the five of you, of course." She spoke also of the burden she'd felt all her life as one touched "so early and so often" by the death of those closest to her. Amazingly, our funeral aunt ended by saying, "Meg, when I

The Funeral Aunt

die, please don't have a regular funeral for me. I've attended enough damn funerals." I began by being shocked, but, in the end, I saw her point, and I promised.

I fell asleep in a *chaise longue* beside her bed, and when I awoke the next morning she was gone. It was the same day on which her father had died lacking only five years of a full century before.

It was fortunate. We all were home for the non-funeral. The four of us were all together at her graveside. Mac said a wonderful prayer, pretty much the same as the one we'd said over Wooly. I asked, "Can we sing?" and Cicely said, "Don't look at me. You know I have no rhythm," which made us laugh. Beth said, "I know just the right one," and proceeded to sing the song from the movie Alice's Restaurant, "Songs to Aging Children." Then all of us remaining aging children trooped back to our "funeral aunt's house" for some hot tea and cake and gave Aunt Lu to God. She taught us very well. LIFE GOES ON.

Grave Humor

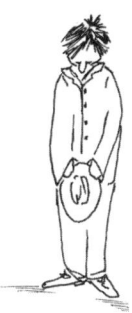

The friendship between Buddy and me goes back over thirty years. We never went out together in the "dating" sense. He was my roommate's boyfriend. He and Monica were an item from their (our) first semester at L.S.U. I got to know him when we double-dated. Monica tried mightily to line me up with someone I could depend on as she depended on Buddy. He was just paternal enough to be attractive to Monica, who had a strong father, and too paternal for me. It worked out well. He came from near Natchitoches in North Louisiana, and he was totally fascinated with all the food, fun, and culture of the southern half of the state. We made many a road trip in Monica's utterly fine car, a Thunderbird convertible. Her family was old sugar money, not that she was in the slightest bit affected by her privilege. Monica was a regular type of girl. She adored dancing and, like Buddy, was a huge fan of monster movies. Their favorites were the "Godzilla" series, and Monica was heard to complain that Buddy insisted they actually watch the movie when he took her to see one at the Tiger Drive-In.

For Easter break, Monica invited us both to stay with her on "the farm," her family's thousand-acre sugar plantation just outside of Thibodaux. She had me set up with dates with her two cousins, older than us, who attended Washington & Lee. We would dance at the College Inn, maybe even go down to "the Island" (Grand Isle) for the day. I was all excited. We began the trip on a sunny, breezy day driving along with the top on the T-Bird down, radio blaring. Down Highway 1 we flew, not a care in the world. Monica drove as far as Donaldsonville, where we stopped among the banana bushes in the parking lot of The First & Last Chance Café for burgers and beer. Then Buddy took the wheel for the second part of the trip.

"I know something fun to do," Monica said as we approached Bayou Lafourche. "Here, Buddy, take the road on the left side of the bayou." She chuckled to herself. "This," she said, "will be better than the Prairieville Light."

Since Monica and I met in September, green little freshmen girls going out for sorority rush and trying to meet football players, we'd discovered that we had lots of likes and dislikes in common. For one thing, we loved to stay up late telling scary stories. We were famous in our dorm. For Hallowe'en, Monica arranged a trip to the haunted houses in New Orleans, and we all made our marks on Marie Laveau's tomb with chalk. Some of the more sober-minded girls from very religious homes were turned off by us, but Monica said we were just back-sliding Methodists having some fun. We didn't go in for voodoo or anything like that, just mild to moderate scare stuff.

Then along came Buddy. They shared this great passion for horror movies, monster movies, anything that got your blood pressure up. I got the dubious honor of being their tag-along. In the very dead of winter we'd gone to sit on a gravel road out in a field near Prairieville because the famous supernatural light that was sometimes seen there had been said to be especially active just then. I had a first date with a fraternity brother of Buddy's, and that poor soul must have thought I was a mental case because I couldn't stop shaking, but it was so cold. Buddy and Monica were really into the atmosphere, so they put the T-Bird's top down, and there we sat with frost forming on us. My date (Rob? Ron? Totally forgettable) and I huddled together for warmth, but he couldn't kiss me because my teeth were chattering. We never saw the damned light, but Buddy and Monica were hysterically funny, keeping up a running commentary for the hours (actually probably forty minutes) we sat there. So if Monica's surprise was the equal of the Prairieville Light, it could be as much of a non-event as that experience, or it could be much fun, as most adventures with the two of them usually turned out to be.

With Buddy asking every five minutes, "Are we close, yet?" like a three-year-old, we sped down the "Back Bayou" road. Leaving Ascension Parish behind, we entered Assumption Parish. Finally, after assuring Buddy one hundred times that, yes, we were close, Monica pointed ahead to a brick church beside the road. "Pull in and park," she commanded.

Churches, especially Roman Catholic churches, were always open in those innocent days. Indeed, we went right in, but not before Monica had given us a stern little admonition to "Behave." Queen of the Ghost Story she might be, but she was not about to incite disrespect in a church.

"Still," she said, "y'all really gotta see this!"

"This" was a glass casket against the north wall of the church near the entrance. The casket was beautifully constructed, and within it lay an effigy. "She's made of wax," Monica hissed, although the church was empty except for the three of us. "She's Ste. Faustine, virgin and martyr. There's supposed to be a little piece of the real saint contained somewhere in there."

"Where?" Buddy enquired, as I said, "Which part?"

"Don't know," was her reply, "but the hair was given as a thank offering for a miracle by some woman who prayed to her. See the wig. It's real hair." That was when we noticed the worst wig ever made, human hair, definitely, but of an auburn-black my mother always referred to as "roachy". It was badly stitched with a center part and sat askew on the saint's wax pate, giving her a slightly rakish appearance. The effect was to render the tragic statue comical, but the worst thing was the pair of copper colored bobby pins that sat, one on each side just above the place where her ears should be. It was just too much. The dim little church was slightly spooky, and the effigy was quite lifelike at first sight.

Grave Humor

Probably we impressionable kids, longing to be scared, had absorbed just enough atmosphere to be hysterical. Whatever it was, we burst out howling with glee, tore out of the church, into the car, and guffawed all the way to Monica's house. The tale was never as funny in the re-telling of it, but it remained our all-time favorite story. We'd fall back on it whenever we encountered anything that was supposed to be serious but seemed to be mostly ridiculous, and the expression, "Ste. Faustine's wig" became our byword for tacky.

The years went by, as years do. Buddy and Monica dated for three years and were supposed to get married but didn't. We all graduated and got jobs. We all got married. Monica was my maid of honor, and I was hers, but she and I have become no more than Christmas correspondents. Buddy and I, on the other hand, never got very far away for very long. Oh, when he was married to his first wife and living in New Orleans and Massachusetts, my Bill and I didn't feel really warm towards her, but we always enjoyed visiting Buddy. He and Bill got along famously, although Bill never has shared our lugubrious pastimes. He is Mr. Outdoors, so we always arranged some kind of hunting or fishing opportunity for him while we went "rou-gon-rou-ing" (Monica's term for our rambling adventures). Over the years, Buddy and I have developed the hobby of exploring cemeteries. This seemed to be a logical outcome of our ghost story obsession in earlier days. I tend to want to find my numerous, scattered relatives' last resting places. He is particularly interested in yellow fever stories. He says he got hooked on this detail while living in New Orleans. He found out that both his paternal great-great grandmothers died of fever in the Great Epidemic of 1853, the worst known in Louisiana, and that his maternal great-grand-mothers both died in the 1873 contagion. He says this has to be some kind of a rare coincidence, so, wherever he goes in the South, he checks out the yellow fever history. I suppose it must be explained here that he is a writer. No one in any other line of work could get away with such arcane pursuits. He married very well the second time, an

Grave Humor

heiress from Shreveport who is an attorney. She loves her work and doesn't mind at all that he writes lots and sells little. Billy and I visit them all the time because we have a camp up near Shreveport. Together Buddy and I have gone to many a cemetery, all over the state and even up East. Lately our focus has been those up in the northwestern part of Louisiana ("Another country entirely," he never fails to remind me.) We went to the little town of Oil City west of Shreveport one Saturday. Oil City, he informed me, is the site of the first off-shore oil derrick, built in 1911 to drill for oil in Caddo Lake. We were not, however, going to the lake. "Wear something kind of nice," Buddy had instructed, "sort of like you were going to a funeral." We did go to a funeral, or at least to a graveside service. It was two in the afternoon, and the voice of the pastor was accompanied by the "chuh-chuh-pook" noises of six oil wells pumping all around the cemetery.

"They only pump three hours a day," Buddy informed me. "Why they always schedule funerals during those hours, I couldn't tell you, but they do."

Grave Humor

He was really excited another time when I came to town expressly to visit "the Yellow Fever Mound," as he called it. "It's in the Catholic Cemetery on the west side of town," he enthused. "It's where they buried the yellow fever victims of the 1873 epidemic. It's on the ridge that was the trail to Texas. Just wait 'til you see." The sign out front seemed to belie some of the story. "This cemetery wasn't even founded until 1883, Buddy," I insisted. "Look at the historical marker." He deflated before my eyes but revived when we got to the rear of the graveyard and saw the impressive monument to the priests who lost their lives ministering to the sick. He was miffed that I insisted on researching further, saying I doubted his facts. He's sensitive that way. After I got the scoop from the priest at Holy Trinity Church, I found out that the bodies of three of the priests were re-interred in the "new" cemetery when it was opened. I wrote it to Buddy. "But don't be dismayed, dear," I concluded. "It's still a juicy story, and besides, I've dragged you all over looking for my relatives. Remember the time I hauled you to Andover, Massachusetts looking for early Phillipses in the graveyard behind Phillips Academy. We found Harriet Beecher Stowe but nary a single ancestor of mine. You didn't fuss at me. You teased me about the abolitionists. If it makes a good story, it's worth the trip, anyway." Whatever the goal, we always have fun on these treks.

Buddy was not to be repressed. He wanted me to know he is the yellow fever expert. "Did you know, " he wrote me shortly thereafter, "that during the epidemics of the nineteenth century unmarried young men were the ones who nursed the sick and dying? It was, of course, because they had no family responsibilities. The priests were just part of this tradition." I deferred to his superior wisdom on that one. I prefer funnier grave stories.

I'd talked forever about our taking a trip to Graceland. Now there would be a burial site to be savored. The Elvis Syndrome in all its glory: just think of it. Buddy wasn't so sure. "I'd be afraid we'd crack up like we did at Ste. Faustine's," he'd say, "and the Elvisians would kill us on the spot."

Grave Humor

Ste. Faustine remained our benchmark, never to be excelled or even equaled in campy appeal, until just this Easter Week. We went up to the northern corner where our cottage is finally taking shape. On Saturday Buddy came to fetch me. "Where are we going?" I asked.

"To see a grave that's better than Ste. Faustine." I could not believe it. I scoffed. That experience has stood the test of over thirty years of silly, sad, and tacky site visits. I was, I have to admit, wrong.

First we went to a dark and smoky barroom near Bossier City, to "get in the mood," Buddy insisted. In the middle of the day the place was full of what we now condescendingly refer to as "blue collar" types. Beer was the beverage of choice, and Hank Williams was on the juke box. It turned out that was an important clue.

"You remember Hank Williams died on New Year's morning of 1953 in the back seat of his car . . ."

"Brand new Cadillac," I interposed. I am something of a minor fan. "It was in Ohio. He was going to do a New Year's Day show . . ."

"But he died. He was writing a song, had the words on a piece of paper in his hand. Anyway, his wife, his first wife, Audrey, the mother of Bocephus, had him buried in Montgomery, Alabama, and twenty-five thousand people came to the funeral."

"And the man who'd just fired him from the Grand Ole Opry because he was always coming drunk to the shows, told his widow, 'Hank would say he'd damn well told us he could draw more fans dead than we could alive!'"

"Yeah, but he actually had two widows. Just before he died, he'd married a nineteen year old named Billie Jean. She was his actual widow, but Audrey ran everything. She'd coached him to fame, she felt like he was hers, and she designed the funeral and his grave marker. Billie Jean was left on the sidelines." Then Buddy finished off his beer and got up. "Come on," he said, "it's time to go see Johnny."

Grave Humor

Johnny Horton is buried near Haughton, Louisiana in Hillcrest Cemetery. You can see his grave as you come in the front gate. "A few years ago, there was a seven foot tall cement guitar covered in red tile here," Buddy informed me, as we approached the grave. "They had to take it down because fans kept defacing it, stealing the tiles." My mouth was, by that time, gaping open.

Johnny Horton, a contemporary of the Great Hank, was killed in an automobile accident in Texas in 1960. He was just coming into his own as a popular singer, having recorded the number one hit of 1959, "The Battle of New Orleans." He also was the author of "North to Alaska," the theme song of the very popular John Wayne movie of the same name. He was on his way, but he died before he could really achieve big success. Like Hank, Johnny Horton was a product of Shreveport's famed Louisiana Hayride, and like Hank, he was promoted and coached by his devoted wife. Today he lies under a monument comprised of one of his autographed guitars surrounded by artificial flowers and encased in a plexiglass case. Black painted rebar, set in cement, holds the whole thing in the ground. It is hard to convey by the written word how wonderfully awful the thing is. Before I could stoop down to read the bronze tablet, Buddy caught my arm and led me to a nearby bench. "I want to read you something, " he said. He extracted a card from his pocket.

"'Hiram "Hank" Williams,'" he read, "'was buried in a silver-lined coffin. He lies in Montgomery's Oakwood Cemetery along with other family members, in a plot his first wife, Audrey, obtained. She designed his monument, which includes a Western style hat on a plinth seven feet tall. A bronze plaque bears his picture, his birth and death dates, and a musical clef showing the first notes to "I Saw the Light," the words of which are also on the plaque.' Now, I want you to look at Johnny Horton's plaque." So I got up and went over to the delicious monstrosity and looked.

There was a bronze tablet below the guitar. It had pine

GRAVE HUMOR

branches embossed on it in bas-relief. It had the name "JOHNNY HORTON" and his dates (1925-1960). It had a treble clef showing one sharp (the key of F,) a "c" indicating 4/4 time, and two notes, a "D" and a "G" as best I could tell. Underneath it was the sentiment: "HERE LIES A PERFECT MAN, MY HUSBAND."

I reeled from the grave howling with glee. "A perfect man, indeed!"

"What's the matter?" Buddy teased. "Aren't you going to put that on Bill's tombstone?"

I declined to even honor that gibe with an answer. "Come on back here," he ordered, gesturing to the cement bench. "Now I shall fill in the blanks. Are you ready?"

"Stop it, Buddy," I shrieked. I could not stop laughing.

"Guess who was Johnny Horton's wife."

"An accomplished liar," I rejoined. I was still dealing with the "perfect man" inscription.

"Billie Jean Williams."

"Hank's . . ."

". . . widow. That's correct. She may not have been allowed to design Hank's final resting place, but she learned from Audrey how to do it up in the best tradition. Here's the proof."

"It really does rank up there with Faustine's wig, doesn't it?"

"Just as tacky, just as sincere."

"The perfect man!"

"Give the poor girl a break. She was only in her twenties. They'd only been married a few years."

"I still can't stand it. On behalf of women everywhere, I protest."

Grave Humor

"It's right there, set in bronze." He always has to get the last word. I always let him.

• • •

We retired to a nearby drugstore to buy one of those disposable cameras so that we could document the sight. "I'm going to send one of the pictures to Monica. She won't believe we finally saw something as wonderful as Ste. Faustine's wig!" We drove home playing Hank and Johnny and Patsy Cline and George Jones as we rode along. In Haughton the sun was setting over the egregious guitar . . . We'd logged another successful expedition to commit to memory and lore. Will we ever top it? We sure will try. The most memorable grave . . . the quest goes on.

COMPASS

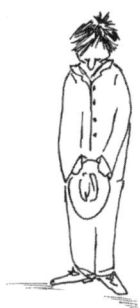

The house is full, guests everywhere, every chair taken and people standing or leaning against the walls, door frames, mantles. I go from room to room, picking up empty cups, plates, glasses, doing the hostess thing. Mac and Mama taught me how to do this when I was little. I have always been the perfect tea girl—and I've had plenty practice. "We entertain," Ma always says. "This family knows how to give a party."

And this is a very successful party. The volume of conversation is exactly that of a interesting blending of guests. There are elderly men (few) and women (many), friends of Mama's. There are relatives. There are younger people, friends of Ron's and mine, people I work with, some he works with, even a few Black friends. It's a big deal, this fête. Everyone is talking. "People like to get together," Ma always says. "It's a public service to give a party and indulge their desire to see and talk with other people." She'd usually use this to spur me on to faster, more thorough silver polishing or some such task. After Nanny died, I was the chief assistant for all her parties, and Nanny has been dead now for twelve years.

Actually, I do have help. There are maids in the kitchen, busy as bees putting food onto platters, into bowls, to go in the dining room where the dining table and buffet are covered with offerings. "Always have plenty of good food," is another Mama rule of entertaining. "I would rather not have a party than have it be stingy." That's us all over. No shortage of food today—or ever. I include the kitchen and dining room in my circuit. Have to make sure everything is going according to the plan. It is.

In the parlor, there are lots of people, but the mood is less festive, more serious. Mama's boss ("As if she ever had a boss!" he teased me when I introduced him that way once), two of my best friends, a man who has come here for the first time and got lost on the way. This is where I came looking for Ma, but she's not here. There's the picture of her, taken on her last birthday. It shows her "counting the loot," gesturing towards the many presents. She's cute, as usual, and the star of the show. Her essence is present, but not her.

I retrace my path, back through the dining room (Folks are still filling plates. This party will go on for a while.), the den, the kitchen where my blessed husband is carving yet another ham. I go out on the back porch but must escape because Ma's two little yappy dogs want to be petted, and they will ruin my stockings. They always do. Out the screen door and down the back steps. I seem to have taken off my shoes. I do that, at parties. Oh, well. It won't be the first pair of ruined stockings I've worn home from one of Mama's "do's."

I open the heavy door of her big Buick coupe and sit in the passenger seat. I smell the "Mama scent", composed of Esteé Lauder's "Youth Dew," chocolate candy, and the faint whiff of old tobacco. She quit smoking—she claims—a year ago, but the tobacco trace still lingers in the car. Ma loves her car, even though she managed to run over herself with it a couple of months earlier. She thought she had it in "PARK", but she didn't, and it knocked her down and rolled over her, crushing her chest. It almost killed her that day. "Ah," she says to me (in my head), "but I lived to drive it again." She calls it "The Murder Weapon."

The tears come then, hot and painful. I've been really brave, so far. I've amazed everyone, especially myself. She really is dead, gone. I can't seem to take it in. I can't find her anywhere. I thought I'd find her here, in The Murder Weapon. She always

Compass

said she felt most comfortable, most at home driving her car. So many of her friends, the older ones, particularly, have said over and over what a blessing it is that Ione died before she got "down" and couldn't drive. I guess that's true, but dammit! Where is she? We've hardly ever been separated, not since she had me just before she turned forty years old and almost died in the process.

Hell! I'm really bawling now, sitting in an otherwise empty car, snatching Kleenex from the box that sits on the seat. I want my Mama. I have totally lost it, me with a huge party going on just a few yards away. The obligations of a hostess were taught to me early and often. ("You can never be rude to a guest in your home, Baby, nor when you are a guest in theirs," Ma would instruct. I inevitably asked, "When, then can I be rude?" only to be told, again and again, "Never." This answer never seemed satisfactory to me.) I produce a tiny laugh thinking of this youthful misapprehension. Then I chuckle outright, as I hear (in my head) Ma say, "That's my Baby. You go on and laugh. You know, Baby, there's never anything so sad that you can't find something funny . . ."

I wipe my eyes as best I can and straighten my silk dress and prepare to rejoin the party. They will know I've been crying, of course, but I'm entitled. At least now I know where she is. She's right where she's always been, in my head and in my heart, and,

Compass

although she's gone from sight, she's never gonna leave me alone. She'll be correcting my behavior and telling me I'm the most beautiful Baby in the world until the day I close my own eyes here and open them to see her again. She's been my compass all the days of my life, and, although she managed to die, she will be my compass yet. There's a party to tend to and a family tradition to uphold. I exit The Murder Weapon and go inside to make Mama proud.